P   ne

Also available in Large Print
by Erle Stanley Gardner:

The Case of the Mischievous Doll
The Case of the Mythical Monkeys
The Case of the Spurious Spinster

Erle Stanley Gardner

THE CASE OF THE
Phantom Fortune

G.K.HALL &CO.
Boston, Massachusetts
1984

Published in Large Print by arrangement with
William Morrow and Company.

British Commonwealth rights courtesy of
Thayer Hobson and Company.

G.K. Hall Large Print Book Series

Set in 16 pt. English Times

Library of Congress Cataloging in Publication Data

Gardner, Erle Stanley, 1889-1970.
  The case of the phantom fortune.

  "Published in large print"—T.p. verso.
  1. Large type books.   I. Title.
[PS3513.A6322P5   1984]   813 '.52   84-12883
ISBN 0-8161-3754-4

THE CASE OF THE
Phantom Fortune

Foreword

SHIGEO OGATA, M.D., an expert in the field of legal medicine whose background fairly bristles with academic honors, received a large part of his training under Dr. Richard Ford, whom I have mentioned from time to time in these forewords. I think that one of Dr. Ford's great satisfactions is the knowledge that men who have been trained by him are having an important effect upon the field of legal medicine throughout the world.

Dr. Ogata has an attitude toward science that is typically Japanese. In the presence of the science which he has made his life work he is as a priest entering a temple. In his search for truth he is always conscious of his great responsibilities and everything is subordinated to his desire to be worthy of the trust that has been placed in him.

He was educated in Japan and then had post-graduate experience at Boston in the United States, England, France, Belgium, the Netherlands, Denmark, West Germany, Austria, Italy and Switzerland. He is at present professor of the

Department of Legal Medicine at the Kyoto Prefectural University of Medicine.

Dr. Ogata says: "When I begin an autopsy, I always pray God in order to obtain an exact answer. If I do this in a humble and pious frame of mind, the cadaver tells me the facts."

It was with this humble attitude that Dr. Ogata performed an autopsy upon a woman who had been found dead in the reeds beside a big river at the foot of a dike.

At first the police felt the woman might have committed suicide. However, the chief of the criminal department of Kyoto police headquarters asked Dr. Ogata to perform an autopsy.

There was nothing by which the body could be identified: no marks on the clothing, no papers, no other means of identification.

Dr. Ogata carefully dissected the corpse, learning, as he did so, many things about the lifetime habits and environment of the woman whose body he was dissecting, her temperament and her mentality. He learned many things from clues which a less able man would have overlooked.

Finally he was able to find out and publicize so much about the habits, background and environment, as well as the mental characteristics of the woman, that a person who had employed this woman as a servant almost a year earlier recognized the description, and upon being shown the body, was able to make an identification.

Using this identification as a starting point, the

police, under Dr. Ogata's direction, were able to find the man who, under the guise of befriending the dead woman, had sought to rob her and had killed her.

Dr. Ogata, having shown by his autopsy that the woman had been murdered, had then gone on beyond the cause of death to find so many clues to the characteristics of the woman in her lifetime that an identification was made purely from his minutely detailed description and the facts pinpointed by his deductive reasoning.

It was a remarkable achievement.

I mention this case in some detail because it is so typical of the work being done by this devoted group of medical specialists who have dedicated themselves to the field of legal medicine.

As a result of what these men learn from the dead, the living can lead their lives in greater security.

And because Dr. Ogata is a typical representative of this group of dedicated experts and because he is so thoroughly humble, with a truly Oriental and devout appreciation of his indebtedness to the Deity, I respectfully dedicate this book to my friend,

SHIGEO OGATA, M.D.

Erle Stanley Gardner

Chapter One

DELLA STREET, Perry Mason's confidential secretary, said, "Mr. Horace Warren, an executive type who seems accustomed to getting what he wants, is anxiously and impatiently waiting in the outer office."

"And what," Perry Mason asked, "does Horace Warren wish to consult me about?"

"That," Della said, "is a mystery."

"Well?" Mason asked. "What's the mystery?"

"All he'll tell me, is that he's willing to pay five hundred dollars to have you attend a buffet dinner tonight."

Mason said, "Tell him I'm not a paid entertainer, that I have a busy schedule today, and that I see clients only by appointment."

"I don't think that he wants you as a social lion," Della said. "He said he would like to have you get a feminine partner of your own choosing, and that he would like to have you observe a certain person and give him your impressions of that person."

1

Mason regarded Della Street thoughtfully. "Were you by any chance thinking of a buffet dinner?"

She nodded. "With champagne," she said.

Mason grinned. "Show Mr. Horace Warren in, Della."

Della Street flashed him a grateful smile, returned to the outer office and a moment later was back with a man somewhere in his late forties; a man with steady gray eyes that flashed out from under bushy eyebrows.

"Mr. Mason," he said, "I'm Horace Warren. I'm a businessman."

Mason smiled slightly. "A student of character would so classify you."

"And you are a student of character?"

"Any trial lawyer likes to think that he is. If he's at all successful he has to be. Won't you be seated?"

Warren sat down across the desk from Mason, regarded him thoughtfully, then leaned forward and put his elbows on the desk. His heavy shoulders and neck gave him an air of belligerency.

"That," he said, "is one of the reasons I came to you."

"What is?"

"That you're a judge of character. I want you to do some judging."

Mason said, "I take it that what you want is a little unusual?"

"Do you," Warren asked abruptly, veering

2

away from the subject under discussion, "have some good detective agency that does your work?"

"Yes," Mason said, "the Drake Detective Agency, with offices on the same floor in this building. Paul Drake has done my work for years. He is highly competent and completely ethical."

"Does he know fingerprints?" Warren asked.

"What do you mean?"

"Can he classify fingerprints and match them, things of that sort?"

"He has had some experience in courtroom cases," Mason said warily. "He's never qualified as a specialist in fingerprinting, but he is an expert and in touch with highly competent experts."

Warren hesitated a moment, then reached into his coat pocket and pulled out a slip of white cardboard. Attached to this cardboard was a strip of transparent tape, and underneath the transparent tape were the black whorls of a fingerprint.

"I want you to hire Paul Drake and have him get busy right away," Warren said. "I want a report by five o'clock this afternoon. It is imperative that I have it by that time."

"Why don't you step down the hall and talk with Mr. Drake yourself?" Mason asked.

"Because I don't want Paul Drake to know who your client is. I want Paul Drake to follow your instructions and yours alone."

"Perhaps," Mason said, "you'd better tell me a little more."

"Tonight," Warren said, "my wife and I are

giving a buffet dinner for a small, intimate group. There will be not more than sixteen or eighteen people. I want you to attend that dinner and bring with you some feminine partner, and I want it to appear that your presence is very casual; in fact, if possible, unexpected.

"The manager of my enterprises, Judson Olney, will ostensibly be the one responsible for bringing you there. Olney will apparently have invited the woman who is with you to come and bring a male escort. You will be the escort she has selected.

"I don't want anyone to suspect you are there in your professional capacity. You will be prepared for a black tie, champagne buffet dinner. You will arrive at seven for cocktails, dinner will be at eight, and you can leave at ten. That will take three hours. I am prepared to pay five hundred dollars for those three hours, in addition to whatever the charge may be for this consultation, and, of course, whatever your costs are for the detective agency."

Mason regarded the enigmatic gray eyes thoughtfully. "I don't like to go at things blind," he said.

"This is not the usual type of case," Warren hastened to assure him.

"So it would seem," Mason told him. "Now, what's all this about a fingerprint and why do you want a detective agency?"

Warren tapped the cardboard on which appeared the lifted fingerprint. "I want your man to find out to whom that fingerprint belongs; that is, who made it."

Mason shook his head.

"What do you mean, no?" Warren demanded.

"What you are asking is a practical impossibility," Mason said. "While the FBI and the police have done wonderful work in matching single fingerprints in the cases of well-known and much-wanted outlaws, nevertheless single fingerprint identification is an exceedingly difficult and tedious job, far beyond the range of any detective agency.

"What is not generally realized is that complete classifications are made through ten fingerprints. Then those fingerprints are broken down into a code so that the searcher using that code is limited to a relatively few number of fingerprints from which to make a match."

"If you had ten fingerprints you could tell who the person was?" Warren asked.

"There again, another factor enters into the picture," Mason said. "*If* the fingerprints of the person in question are on file in the criminal side of the FBI, we could get some police officer to make an inquiry for us by wire and get a match. If, however, the fingerprints are not on file *in the criminal department,* it would probably be impossible because fingerprints which are filed for civilian identification are considered confidential."

Warren nodded, his eyes half closed as though contemplating some matter entirely disassociated with what Mason was saying.

Then abruptly he got to his feet, took a billfold from his pocket, extracted a check and handed it to Mason.

"Here," he said, "is a check for a thousand dollars. Five hundred dollars will cover your attendance at dinner tonight. I have given the address to your secretary. The other five hundred dollars will act as retainer.

"Now, in strictest confidence I am going to give you some additional data on that fingerprint."

"It is always advisable to give an attorney all the facts," Mason said dryly.

Warren said, "This fingerprint may have been made by one of the servants in my house, it may have been made by one of the guests who will be at the dinner tonight, or it *may* be that it was made by a total stranger. Would it be possible for your man, Drake, to go through the house and get the fingerprints of the servants without their knowing it? I believe you refer to it as developing latent prints."

Mason shook his head. "I don't think that would be possible, and if you don't want Drake to know the identity of my client it wouldn't be at all feasible.

"Developing a latent print, Mr. Warren, is a matter which calls for the use of various colored powders which are dusted over the fingerprint. Then the developed fingerprint has to be photographed or, as was done in the case of the fingerprint here, lifted."

"Lifted?" Warren asked. "How is that done?"

"The fingerprint is dusted. Then transparent adhesive tape is placed over the dusted latent fingerprint. The adhesive tape is smoothed carefully so that it covers the entire surface, then it is peeled back off and placed upon a card having an appropriate color so that the fingerprint will show in contrast.

"For instance, on this card which you have handed me, the fingerprint was dusted with a graphite powder; therefore the print, after it was lifted, was placed upon a card with an off-white background, which makes it readily visible.

"Now, if Drake were to go to your house and start lifting fingerprints, he would have to dust various surfaces and it would be virtually impossible to remove evidence that he had dusted those surfaces, and complete his search within the allotted time."

"Have you any suggestions?" Warren asked.

"I have one," Mason said. "It might or might not prove effective. It would, however, necessitate Drake knowing the identity of my client and it would be expensive."

"Money is no object," Warren declared. "That is, I don't want to be a pigeon, I don't want to be charged more than the going rate, but when I want something, I want it."

Mason nodded thoughtfully.

"What was your scheme?"

Mason said, "Have a caterer for this party. Ostensibly, Drake will be the head of the catering service.

"In that way the service will furnish its own china, its own crystal, its own silverware. Employees of the catering firm will park a truck in your driveway. That truck will be the head-quarters of the catering service. Apparently dishes, glassware, silverware, etc., will be taken from your house to the truck to be washed. Actually there will be no washing facilities available but there *will* be an unlimited supply of glassware and silverware, which will be replaced from time to time as occasion demands.

"This catering truck will actually be a portable fingerprint laboratory in which Drake will have assistants who will develop latent fingerprints on glasses, silverware, etc., as fast as the materials are brought out."

"How much would something of this sort cost?" Warren asked.

"It is expensive," Mason said. "How many guests do you intend to have at your party?"

"Fifteen," Warren said, "if they all come. My wife and I will make seventeen, and you and your friend will make nineteen."

"And what did you intend to serve?"

Warren said, "Champagne, filet mignon, hors d'oeuvres, the works."

"Catering alone," Mason said, "would probably cost you twenty-five to thirty-five dollars a person. This dummy caterer's truck, which is really a fingerprint laboratory with several trained assistants, costs five hundred dollars for an evening, in addition to the catering charge."

"It's available?" Warren asked.

"It's available unless some other detective agency has it tied up for this evening. It is, of course, a very hush-hush service. The public generally knows nothing about it. It is held in readiness for private detective agencies who are confronted with a problem somewhat similar to the one we are discussing."

"Get it," Warren said.

"Just a minute," Mason said.

He nodded to Della Street, who picked up the telephone and dialed Paul Drake's number.

When he had the detective on the line Mason said, "Paul, I have a very confidential fingerprint job I want done tonight. The suspect may or may not be a guest at a champagne buffet dinner. Can you arrange to get the fingerprint truck for tonight?"

"I don't know," Drake told him, "but I can find out pretty fast."

"Find out and call me back," Mason said.

"I'll run it down and let you know," Drake said.

"That's fine," Mason told him, and then putting a little more emphasis on the words, said, "find out and *call me back* just as soon as you get the information, Paul."

"I got you," Drake said. "I gottcha the second time anyway. I was a little dense the first time. I'm to keep away from the office and report by telephone. Right?"

"Right," Mason said, and hung up.

Mason turned to his client. "We'll find out in a few minutes whether it's available."

"Now, let me emphasize one thing," Warren said. "This is a business party and I want the catering to be very high class. I don't want some detective agency bungling the—"

"The detective service is entirely beside the point," Mason said. "The catering is in the hands of a professional. The detective end is a sideline carried on in one end of the truck. You will, of course, have to have your driveway kept open so that the truck can park there. Trained servants who are taught to put everything on trays will take the things to the house and see that they are not touched except by guests and by your own servants. Then those articles will be removed and sent to the truck, ostensibly to be washed. Actually they will be given the closest fingerprint examination by well-trained assistants.

"There may be inquiries about the catering service. You will have to say that you hired them because of a recommendation by a friend, and of course under no circumstances can any guest go to the truck to look around."

Warren nodded.

"Now then," Mason said, "specifically what do you want me to do? Suppose we locate this fingerprint. What then? Do you simply want me to advise you of the identity of the person and withdraw, or—"

"No," Warren said, "I've been thinking things over. You'll have to be on your own for a while.

There are certain reasons why it's going to be rather difficult for me to be in professional communication with you, Mason.''

"There's always the telephone," Mason said.

"Unfortunately I have very few moments when people are not with me," Warren said. "I have a secretary in charge of appointments. I have a rather elaborate staff.''

"Perhaps I can telephone you," Mason said, "and we could handle a conversation in such a way that the comments made at your end of the line would seem to relate to some business matter. In that way I could give you the information—"

"No, no. My calls have to pass through a switchboard in the office and . . . I'm going to turn you loose on your own, Mason.''

"Just what do you want?" Mason asked.

"That fingerprint that you have," Warren said. "I want you to find out who made that fingerprint. When you find out who made it, I want you to protect my wife against that person. You understand, Mason? No matter who that person may be, no matter how much it may cost in the way of a legitimate fee, I want you to protect my wife from that person.''

"In other words," Mason said, "you're reasonably certain that after tonight I'll know who made that fingerprint. You think the person will be at the buffet dinner.''

"I think the person will be at the buffet dinner.''

"And you want me to protect your wife

against that person."

"Yes."

"What measures do I take?"

"Any measures that may be necessary."

"How much expense do I incur?"

"Any expense within reason. Any expense that you can justify as a reasonable expense will be unhesitatingly paid by me."

"Up to what limit?" Mason asked curiously.

"There is no limit."

"Suppose it should run into several thousands of dollars?"

"I said there is no limit."

"You have a feeling that your wife is in danger?"

"I think," Warren said, "that my wife is either in the clutches of a blackmailer or is about to fall into the clutches of a blackmailer."

Mason raised his eyebrows. "Legitimate law-abiding citizens are seldom subject to blackmail unless, of course, there is something in the past of such a person that would leave him vulnerable, and I take it that in the case of your wife . . ."

"Take what?" Warren asked irascibly, as Mason's voice trailed into silence.

"That there would hardly be such a past."

"Why not?" Warren rasped.

"Surely," Mason said, "with your social and business position, any woman whom you have married would hardly—"

"Stop it!" Warren snapped.

"Stop what?" Mason asked.

"Stop fishing for information under the guise of paying me a lot of compliments and putting me in a position where I'll have to make a statement.

"I'm going to make one statement, Mason. It's the only statement you'll get out of me. The fact that Lorna is my wife doesn't mean a damned thing."

"How long have you been married?" Mason asked.

"We've been married for ten years. It's been a happy marriage, but she is ten years younger than I am. When I married her I was a successful businessman—not a wealthy businessman, but a reasonably successful businessman. I didn't inquire into her past. I married her because I loved her."

"And because she loved you?" Mason asked.

"I don't know," Warren said. "A man never does. I have sometimes thought she married me because she found in me a refuge. I don't know. And because I have never asked her, I don't intend to ask you. I don't want you to tell me anything you might find out about her past or her frame of mind, present or past.

"I am retaining you for just one thing. Protect my wife from the person who made that fingerprint. Don't tell me a damned thing about what you find out. Just go ahead and protect her and from time to time send me the bill for what you feel your services are worth."

"That's a rather difficult assignment," Mason said.

13

"I think you specialize in difficult assignments. I've looked you up one side and down the other."

The unlisted telephone rang. Della Street answered, said, "Thank you, Paul," and hung up.

She caught Mason's eye and nodded.

Mason said, "The catering truck is available for tonight."

"Good!" Warren exclaimed.

Mason regarded the man thoughtfully.

"What makes you think your wife is in danger?" he asked.

"My wife," Warren said, "is being black-mailed."

"How do you know?"

"First the tip-off came from my banker. She has been making withdrawals for a period of more than ninety days. Those withdrawals are large and are in the form of cash."

"And you think she has been paying those over to some blackmailer?"

"No, I know she hasn't."

Mason raised his eyebrows.

"To date she has drawn out something like forty-seven thousand dollars," Warren said, "and as late as last night she had that forty-seven thousand dollars intact in a locked suitcase in her bedroom."

"The entire sum?" Mason asked.

"The entire sum."

"How do you know?"

"I made it my business to find out."

"Then," Mason said, "there is another possibility, which is—"

"I know, I know," Warren interrupted. "Which is that my wife is in love with someone else and is intending to run away and leave me.

"Lorna wouldn't do that. Lorna consented to be my wife ten years ago. At the time there was something bothering her. I know that much. She came from New York, she has never talked about her past, she has never introduced me to a single friend who knew her before she was married. Every friend she has in the world, apparently, is someone with whom she became acquainted after our marriage."

"In other words, her past is something of a mystery?"

"Her past is a closed book," Warren said. "She'd probably tell me if I asked her. I wouldn't ask her. What you were talking about is whether she was planning to run away and leave me. I'm simply telling you Lorna wouldn't do that. She made her bargain. She'd stay with it if it killed her.

"If something happened and she became utterly miserable in our marriage, she might take an overdose of sleeping pills. I don't know. I want to see that that doesn't happen."

"If what you suspect is true," Mason said, "I may have to invent some excuse to see a good deal of your wife."

"Then go ahead and invent the excuse."

"And what you want me to do is to—"

15

Warren interrupted. "Protect my wife from the person who made that fingerprint."

"At all costs?" Mason asked.

"At all costs, at any cost. There is no limit, but I want her protected from the person who made that fingerprint. I will expect your detective's catering service to be prepared to serve an excellent champagne buffet dinner tonight, and I will expect you to be there with some eminently suitable woman who can—"

Mason nodded toward Della Street. "I would have Miss Street with me," he said.

"That's fine," Warren said. "Now, the only person who might even faintly suspect there may be a business relationship will be Judson Olney. He will assume the responsibility for your secretary being there, and she will invite you to accompany her. Since you are rather well known, it might occur to him that there is some logical reason for you to be there.

"Olney will adopt the position of having been a friend of long standing of your secretary, here; and since he is a bachelor this will cause no complications.

"He is, I may add," Warren said, "a *very* eligible bachelor."

"And Olney will know what he has to do?"

"Olney will only know that he has to invite your secretary, Miss . . ."

"Della Street," Mason said.

Warren took a notebook from his pocket, made a note of the name.

16

"All that Judson will know is that he is to invite Miss Della Street to the dinner as an old friend, and introduce her as such. You will be there simply as Miss Street's escort."

"Do you think that will fool anyone?" Mason asked.

"I don't give a damn whether it does or not," Warren said. "I can't think of anything else on short notice that will work any better. In my business I try to plan my activities in the best way available at the moment and then quit worrying about what may happen. After I have decided on a course of action I go ahead—full speed. I don't waste time looking back over my shoulder.

"Now, since this is the last time I will see you before you arrive at my home, we have to be sure that we don't get our wires crossed. Do you have any questions?"

"No," Mason said.

Warren looked at his watch. "I have already used much more than my allotted time. I am going to have to make excuses to account for the delay in my appointment schedule."

He pushed back his chair, got to his feet, started for the door, turned, faced Mason, and said, "No matter who that person may be, you are to protect my wife from the person who made the fingerprint on that card."

After the door had clicked shut, Della Street looked at Perry Mason. "Intrigue," she said. "I love it."

Mason was frowningly studying the fingerprint on the card.

"Think Drake can match it?" she asked.

"If the person who made it is there tonight," Mason said thoughtfully, "Drake should be able to make a match. Unless, of course, the person becomes suspicious and manages to avoid leaving prints."

"Suspicious?" she asked.

"Because I am there," Mason said.

Della said, "Well, if I am to be escorted to a champagne dinner with the four hundred tonight, I should spend what time I can get during the noon hour at the beauty shop."

"Take what time you need," Mason said. "This is business, you know."

Della Street picked up the phone, asked for an appointment at the hairdresser's, said, "Just a moment, please," and turned to Perry Mason. "They can take me now if I can come right away."

"Go ahead," Mason said. "And charge the bill as part of the expense on the case. This is an official assignment, you know."

She said into the phone, "Okay, I'll be right down," hung up and turned to Mason. "Somehow I feel rather . . . well . . . ."

Mason laughed. "You never feel self-conscious when you work until midnight, Della, or when you are called on to work over a weekend. Go ahead and get the works."

Chapter Two

IT WAS nearly two o'clock when a radiant Della Street returned from the beauty shop.

"How do I look?" she asked, standing in front of Perry Mason, and turning slowly.

"Like a million," Mason said.

"I don't want you to be ashamed of me at that buffet dinner."

"Ashamed!" Mason exclaimed. "You'll be the queen of the—"

The telephone bell rang three short, sharp rings which was the switchboard operator's signal that in the outer office there was something urgent and demanding immediate attention. A moment later Gertie, the switchboard operator and receptionist, appeared in the door of the private office.

She carefully closed the door behind her and said, "There's a Mr. Judson Olney out there who wants to see Miss Della Street on a personal matter of some urgency. He wants to see her *alone*."

"My boy friend," Della said.

"Your *what?*" Gertie asked, her eyes growing large and round.

"Only temporarily," Della Street said, smiling. "I'll go out and greet him."

Gertie backed out of the office.

"I want to look him over," Mason said to Della Street, "provided you can arrange it."

"I'll arrange it," she told him.

Della vanished through the door to the outer office.

A few moments later Mason's phone rang and when the lawyer picked up the receiver he heard Della on the other end of the line.

"Where are you, Della?" he asked.

"In the outer office," she said. "I'm talking where he can't hear me."

"Go ahead."

"There's something rather strange here. He didn't want to see anyone except me, but after we'd talked a little while he asked who my escort was going to be and I told him it would be you. That seemed to bother him for a minute and then he said, well, perhaps he was getting a little out of line. I can see that now he knows I'm going with you he wants to meet you, but he's all worked up about something, under some sort of terrific tension."

"See if he wants to come in and meet me," Mason said. "If he does, bring him in."

"I'm satisfied he does. You may expect us in about two minutes," Della said.

However, it was less than a minute after Mason

had terminated the telephone conversation that the door opened and Della said, "Mr. Mason, this is Judson Olney. He's manager of the Warren Enterprises."

Olney, a strapping young man with a ready smile and an air of breezy informality about him, came forward to acknowledge the introduction and take Mason's hand.

"Hello, Mr. Mason," he said. "I'm sorry I bothered you but Della here told me you were going to be her escort tonight and I wanted to drop in and say hello.

"Della and I are old friends from high school days. I was a senior when she was a freshman but I had my eye on her even then. . . . We drifted apart and I lost track of her."

"How did you happen to find her?" Mason asked, his face without expression.

"Simplest way on earth," Olney said. "I was walking down the street yesterday and she drove by. I recognized her. I saw her turn into a parking place nearby, so as I walked past I spoke to the attendant, told him that I'd like to know whether a Miss Della Street was a regular customer of his, and he told me she kept a parking space by the month, that he understood she worked in the office of Perry Mason, the attorney.

"So," Olney said, smiling, "that's the story. I could have made quite a mystery out of it and built myself up as a super detective, but somehow I always like to tell the truth."

His steady blue eyes met Mason's with every

semblance of frankness.

"And that's the truth?" Mason asked.

Della Street caught Judson Olney's eye and shook her head.

Olney grinned sheepishly. "All right," he said, "that's a story I made up. Actually I was instructed by my employer, Horace Warren, to concoct a story which would account for a long friendship with Miss Street, and to invite her as my friend to a buffet dinner tonight. On the other hand, I wasn't to have it appear that there had been anything more than an old friendship which had been dormant for some time and was now being resurrected. So I was therefore instructed to ask Miss Street to bring an escort. She tells me that you are going to take her."

Mason nodded.

"All right," Olney said, "I'm going to be telling that story about Della Street, the old school days and the parking lot and I wanted to rehearse it a little bit."

"Couldn't you do a little better?" Mason asked.

"No," Olney said. "I had a better story but it would have been vulnerable to checking."

"You think someone will check it?" Mason asked.

Olney said cautiously, "I don't know. I want to be safe. I'm being purposely kept in the dark. I don't know what it's all about. I'm told what to do and I'm simply following instructions. I was told to concoct a story that would stand checking."

"That's all you know?" Mason asked.

"That's all I know," Olney said. "But I do want to say one thing on my own."

"What's that?"

"Whatever is in the wind," Olney said, his face suddenly serious, his eyes hard, "had better be on the up-and-up as far as Lorna Warren is concerned."

Mason raised his eyebrows. "You have some particular interest in seeing that her rights are protected?"

"Nothing like that," Olney said. "Well, wait a minute, I have, too. Lorna Warren is one of the sweetest, nicest individuals I've ever met; calm, quiet, patient, considerate, and she treats us folks in the office just fine.

"Now then, it suddenly occurs to me that there's a reason for all this rigmarole I'm supposed to go through, and it *may* be that Horace Warren isn't interested in having Miss Street there but is interested in having *you* there. I hope you don't mind if I put the cards right on the table, sir."

"Go right ahead," Mason invited.

"Horace Warren is my employer. I am loyal to him in a business way. His wife, Lorna, is something very, very special. Don't get me wrong, Mr. Mason. My feelings toward her are simply the feelings of every man and woman in the office. We like Horace Warren. We absolutely idolize Lorna. I would certainly resent being called upon

23

to assist in making it possible for an attorney to be present at that buffet dinner tonight if the ultimate objective of the attorney was to do something which would inconvenience Lorna Warren in any way."

"You are now waiting for a statement from me?" Mason asked.

"I am waiting for a statement from you."

Mason said, "I have no official connection with either Horace Warren or Lorna Warren which would cause me to do anything against the best interests of Lorna Warren."

Olney's face lit up. "Well, now *that's* something," he said. "That makes me feel a lot better. . . . Well, there's no use keeping up the pretense with you folks. You'll be there, I understand, at seven. Do I rate the privilege of giving you a platonic kiss on the cheek, Miss Street? After all, you were the proud, unattainable beauty when we were both in high school."

"When you were a senior and she was a freshman?" Mason asked.

Olney made a little grimace. "That part of the story," he said, "doesn't hang together so well when you pick it up with that lawyer's tone of polite sarcasm."

"Why use it then?"

"It's the only story that will stand investigation."

"And you were told there might be an investigation?"

24

"I was told to get a story which couldn't be shown false on its face. I obey orders."

Della Street said mischievously. "In view of our old school-day association and your fervent, undeclared passion, which you managed to conceal so successfully, you rate a kiss on the cheek and we will do a little babbling about the old days and some of the teachers."

"That's fine," Olney said. "I just wanted to drop in to talk over the ground rules with you and plan it so things would go smoothly tonight."

He bowed, smiled, started for the door, paused in the doorway to turn and size up Perry Mason. The smile left his face.

"I wish I knew what this was all about," he said.

Mason said. "Just a moment, Olney. That story of yours, I don't like it. . . . Can't you think up a better one?"

Olney came back into the room, stared thoughtfully at the floor for a moment. Suddenly he snapped his fingers. "I've got it!" he exclaimed. "A boat trip! Four years ago I went through the Caribbean, then down to South America . . . moonlight dances on deck, warm spice-scented air— Wonderful! *That's* where I met you, Miss Street."

Della flashed Olney a smile.

Mason looked dubious but refrained from commenting until Olney had bowed himself out of the office, then he regarded Della Street thoughtfully. "Your old friend," he said, "is either a good actor or a rotten liar."

Della Street, eyes sparkling, said, "I presume that means you'll ask Paul Drake to be sure to get the fingerprints of Judson Olney tonight?"

"Exactly," Mason said.

Chapter Three

WARREN'S HOUSE at 2420 Bridamoore Street was ablaze with lights. The house was set well back from the road, and the semicircular driveway leading to the front door was wide enough to furnish ample room for parking cars.

On the west side of the house and opening from the driveway was a wide lane leading to a three-car garage.

Perry Mason, slowing his car, glanced at Della Street and said, "Notice the driveway is fairly well filled with parked cars, Della, yet *we're* right on time. Usually guests come straggling in at about any time which suits their convenience."

"What significance is attached to that?" she asked.

"It was planned that way," Mason said. "He wanted all the other guests to be here when we arrived."

Della Street said, "Oh-oh! Look in the driveway to the garage by the side door."

"I noticed it," Mason said. "The big

27

catering van."

"But notice the sign," she said. *"Drake's Catering Service."*

Mason nodded. "The name is painted on heavy paper which fits into a frame. The rest of the sign is permanently painted. In that way they can change the name to suit the occasion. We'll have to kid Paul Drake about the service."

"Something new for Paul," she said, "being a caterer."

"Well," Mason said, turning the car into the driveway, "it seems that we enter from the east and find ourselves a parking place on the left-hand side of the driveway. This house was evidently built with the idea of entertainment in mind."

"A house of headaches," Della Street said. "It takes lots of servants to run a place of this sort and getting domestic help these days is a *real* headache."

Mason parked the car, got out and held the door open for Della Street. "Well," he said, "in we go and try to play the part of innocent bystanders in a script which has been written by a rank amateur."

"You think anyone will suspect anything?" Della asked.

Mason said, "It depends on who's present, Della, but if this is an intimate group that has been together from time to time, and I rather fancy it is, the presence of an attorney and his attractive secretary will cause considerable comment, a great deal of speculation, and if a guilty person is present he won't be deceived for more than ten seconds."

"Yes," Della Street said, as they walked up to the front door, "I can imagine a blackmailer putting the bite on Mrs. Warren and then attending a party at which a noted attorney is introduced as one of the guests. It might be a good thing at that, Chief. It might frighten him out of any plans he might have for a shake-down."

"It *might,*" Mason said dubiously, pressing the button which caused chimes to sound in the interior.

The door was flung open by Judson Olney.

"There you are!" he exclaimed, taking both of Della Street's hands. "I've been waiting for you."

He turned to Perry Mason. "And this is . . . ?"

"Mr. Mason," Della said; then turning her face to Perry Mason, "My old friend, Judson Olney, Chief. I told you about him this afternoon."

"Oh yes," Mason said, shaking hands. "How are you, Mr. Olney?"

Olney expressed his pleasure, then half turned toward the couple who were standing in the reception hall. "Lorna," he said, "this is the girl I was telling you about. Mrs. Warren, Della. And may I present Mr. Mason. —Mrs. Warren, Mr. Mason. And this is Horace Warren, our host. Della Street and Mr. Mason."

Mrs. Warren said, "Welcome. It's certainly a pleasure! Judson told me all about meeting his cruising companion and said you were more beautiful than ever, and now I can well believe it. Judson, you aren't very smart to lose track of a young woman like this."

Olney knocked his head with his knuckles. "Pure ivory," he said.

Warren regarded Mason thoughtfully. "Haven't I seen you someplace before?" he asked.

Mason looked him in the eyes, said, "Have you?"

Warren's brow puckered thoughtfully. "I've seen you or—Wait a minute, I've seen a picture of you. . . . Mason, Mason, why you're *Perry* Mason, the lawyer."

"That's right," Mason acknowledged gravely.

"Well, *what* do you know," Warren exclaimed, awe and respect in his voice.

"Perry Mason!" his wife ejaculated. "Oh-oh! *Perry Mason* in person! Wait until my guests hear about *this?* Well, this *is* something.

"Let me take your things," Lorna Warren said to Della, "and come in and meet these people. It's a rather small intimate group."

Horace Warren moved over to take Mason's arm. "Well, well," he said, "the great Perry Mason. This is indeed an honor, Mr. Mason."

"Thank you," the lawyer said dryly.

In the big living-room area half a dozen people were chatting together, casually holding cocktail glasses. Through huge picture windows there could be seen a swimming pool illuminated by

30

colored globes beneath the surface and by an indirect illumination above the surface which gave the effect of soft moonlight to the wide cement apron and the grass which bordered it.

Another eight or ten persons were standing in groups or spread out in reclining chairs around the pool.

The sound of a dozen voices talking at once, interspersed with occasional feminine laughter, greeted the ears of Mason and Della Street as they entered the room.

Horace Warren stepped to the microphone of a hi-fi player and tape recorder and threw a switch which turned it into a public address system.

"Ladies and gentlemen, I have an announcement to make," Warren said.

From the manner in which people looked up with smiles of amusement, Mason gathered that Warren liked to hear his voice over the public address system and quite frequently made announcements.

"This," Warren said, "is a romantic story, a story involving my right-hand assistant, Judson Olney, who met a beautiful girl while he was on that South American cruise a few years ago, and then lost track of her. Then, quite by accident, he found her again and with Mrs. Warren's permission has invited her here tonight.

"He was gratified to find that this very pretty girl whom he had always visualized as one of the Hollywood stars and who had been a woman of mystery on the cruise, was working in a law office

31

as a confidential secretary. Because Judson is going to be occupied with business matters during a part of the evening, he asked this young woman to bring an escort of her own choosing. She chose her employer, and her employer, ladies and gentlemen—hold everything now—her employer is none other than the famous attorney, the one and only—the great Perry Mason! The young woman is the beautiful Miss Della Street. And here they are! Step forward, please."

Warren held out his hand, and Della Street and Mason stepped forward just as someone pressed a switch on a spotlight.

Warren still held the microphone. "Let's give the newcomers a big hand," he said.

People dutifully looked around for a place to put their cocktail glasses, then broke into spattering applause. The spotlight went off.

Warren turned to Mason and said, "I hate formal introductions where you go around from person to person and group to group. I make many introductions over a loud-speaker. Now, if you will just mingle around, people will give you their names and you can get them catalogued. But first you must have a cocktail."

Mason said, "You have a very remarkable voice, Mr. Warren. That was a smooth, almost professional job you did in the announcement."

Warren's face flushed with genuine pleasure. "Do you think so?" he said. "Thank you, very much."

"I'm quite certain," Mason said, "you must

have had professional coaching."

Warren failed to take the bait. "Come this way and have a cocktail. We have a catering service that is doing a real job."

Warren led the way over to a portable bar where an impassive waiter took their orders, then lifted the lid from an insulated container.

"Look at this," Warren said. "The cocktail glasses are cooled almost to the freezing point. What is your pleasure?"

"Both Miss Street and I would like Scotch-on-the-rocks," Mason said.

The attendant took metal tongs, extracted glasses, put the glasses on a tray, put in ice cubes, poured in Scotch and gravely extended the tray.

Della Street took a glass gingerly, apparently conscious of the fact that in touching the glass she left fingerprints.

Mason took the other glass.

"Now, if you'll excuse me," Warren said, "I have a telephone call I have to make. Just make yourselves right at home. People are friendly here and it's all an informal group."

Mason said, "Could you give me a guest list?"

"I have had one already prepared for you," Warren said. "I thought you'd want one. One for you and one for your charming secretary."

Warren, somewhat surreptitiously, pressed a folded slip of paper into Mason's hand, turned and slipped one to Della Street.

"How's the catering service?" Mason asked.

"Wonderful," Warren enthused. "Really it's

out of this world. I hadn't realized it would be possible to have anything of this sort. . . . And now, if you'll excuse me, I have a couple of telephone calls to make."

Warren started away, turned, caught Mason's eye, gave him a quick wink and jerked his head in a signal that Mason was to follow.

Mason said in a low voice to Della Street, "I'll leave you to your own resources for a little while."

Still carrying his glass, Mason moved over to join Warren.

Warren said, "There's a shower out by the swimming pool. To the right of the shower there's a door leading to a bathroom. That door will be unlocked. Meet me there alone in about five minutes, or whenever you can make it. Pretend that you're just exploring around. Go out and look the house over. Move around the pool. Leave your secretary free to circulate around."

"People will be talking to me," Mason said, glancing at his watch. "It's going to be a little difficult to—"

"That's all right. I'll be waiting. I want to show you something."

Judson Olney came up to take Della Street's arm. "My gosh," he said, "it's good to see you again! You shouldn't have stepped out of my life the way you did."

"It was *you* who stepped out of *my* life," Della reminded him.

Mrs. Warren, moving up, said, "Shame on

34

you, Judson, letting a good-looking girl like that get away."

Olney put his arm around Della Street's shoulders, drew her momentarily close to him, said, "She hasn't got away—yet. Come on, we've got to meet people."

Perry Mason moved out to the swimming pool, pausing every few seconds to shake hands with people who came up to introduce themselves, trying to avoid getting involved in conversation.

After several minutes the lawyer moved around the swimming pool, looking admiringly at the house.

Nearly ten minutes elapsed before he had a chance to open the door to the right of the shower without making the action seem conspicuous.

The door opened into a sumptuous bathroom with a sunken tile tub, huge mirrors.

Horace Warren was waiting.

"I want you to see something with your own eyes," he said.

Warren opened the left-hand door of the bathroom's two doors and beckoned Mason to follow him.

"Now this," Warren said, "is my wife's bedroom. We have separate bedrooms. I'm a restless sleeper and sometimes I'll place a dozen phone calls in the course of an evening. My room is soundproof and this room is pretty well insulated."

"Now, just a moment," Mason said, "I feel rather—well, I'm a little embarrassed about this.

Your wife doesn't know you're here, that you're showing me anything?"

"Heavens, no! I just want you to see this with your own eyes. Just take a look."

Warren led the way to a huge closet, slid back the end door, reached in, took out a locked suitcase.

"Of course," he said, "almost any key will open one of these."

Warren inserted a key, snapped back the lock and the two hasps on the side which held it shut.

"Now just take a look in here," he said, "and . . ."

Warren recoiled in surprise. "Good heavens!" he exclaimed.

The interior of the suitcase was filled with old newspapers.

"Now, what the hell!" Warren said.

"That's what you wanted me to see?" Mason asked.

"Definitely not! Up to a short time ago this suitcase had forty-seven thousand dollars in twenties, fifties, and one-hundred dollar bills."

"You counted it?" Mason asked.

"I counted it."

"Do you think there's any possibility someone could have stolen it?"

"I don't know what *did* happen to it."

"All right," Mason said tersely, "here's a way to have a showdown. Take that receptacle out to the van. Get the experts out there to dust it for fingerprints. Find whose fingerprints are on it."

"Mine are on it now," Warren said.

"Yours and probably someone else's," Mason said.

"But my wife's fingerprints will also be on it."

"Hers and someone else's."

Warren shook his head. "I don't want to do it."

"Why?"

"She'd be apt to come here and miss the suitcase and even after I brought it back she might find that it had been fingerprinted. You said yourself that lifting fingerprints left a trace."

"They can oil that leather after they get done so it won't leave a trace," Mason said. "The prints will be on the metal fittings."

"No," Warren said, "I don't want to take a chance of her catching me at it. I'd have trouble getting it out of the house."

"There's a back way out, isn't there?"

"Yes."

"You could use that."

"But suppose she should come into the bedroom, looking for the suitcase and find it's gone? Then what?"

"Then," Mason said, "you could have a showdown with your wife. You could tell her what you're doing and tell her you're trying to protect her."

"Never," Warren said emphatically, abruptly closing and locking the suitcase. He put it back in the closet and slid the door into place.

"Unless my wife chooses to confide in me," he

said, "I don't want to force the issue. I did want you to see the money for yourself. I guess now the blackmailer has got in his dirty work."

"Your wife has enough money of her own so she could make a payment of that sort?" Mason asked.

"She's been converting securities during the last ninety days that I know of and perhaps even before that. Yes, she's got enough to make that payment and if she converted all of her securities she could make several such payments. I believe in financial independence for both parties to a marriage, Mr. Mason. For your information, I've been generous with my wife and I've been rather successful in a business way." He waved his hand in an inclusive gesture. "As you can see from the sort of place we live in. . . . I wouldn't have Lorna dream that I'd been snooping around in here or that I had confided in you . . . or that you—Come on, let's get out of here."

Mason said, "Very well," and started following Warren toward the door of the bathroom.

Abruptly a door opened and Lorna Warren stood on the threshold, a look of startled, incredulous surprise on her face.

Her husband came to an abrupt halt for a moment, then said casually, almost too suavely, "I'm showing Perry Mason through the house, dear. I took the liberty of just looking in on your bedroom."

Warren turned to Mason and went on easily, "Now, my bedroom is on the other side here. We can reach it either through the bathroom or through the corridor. I have another bath opening off my room. . . . Right this way, please."

Lorna Warren stood to one side.

"When you're finished, dear," she said, "the caterer wants to know about serving the meal. There's a charcoal broiler in the catering van and he wants to have about twenty minutes' advance notice."

"That's fine," Warren said easily. "Tell him to go ahead and get things ready to serve. We should be about ready to start the buffet in twenty minutes."

"They've already brought in the canapés," she said.

"Fine, fine," Warren said. "It's a nice job of catering. Now, right this way, Mr. Mason, and I'll show you the rest of this wing. The guest bedrooms are in the other wing."

Out in the corridor Warren turned to Mason. "Gosh," he said under his breath, *"that* was close! Think what would have happened if we'd been carrying that suitcase."

"What would have happened?" Mason asked.

"I shudder to think of it," Warren told him. "It would have put me in the position of having to make explanations."

"It would also have put your wife in the position of having to make explanations," Mason said. "If you're going to protect a person it helps a lot to know the source of the danger and—"

"No, no, Mason," Warren interrupted, "that

would have defeated the entire object of calling you in. I want this handled in such a way that Lorna doesn't have any idea on earth that you're here other than as a casual guest, and I don't want her to know that I suspect a thing about her financial problem."

"All right," Mason said, "you're calling the shots, but quite obviously if she's being black-mailed she's made one payment of approximately forty-seven thousand dollars. It's too late to protect her from that."

"I know, I know, but the money is a minor matter," Warren said. "I want you to protect her from the blackmailer or whatever it is she's facing, and this is probably the last time we'll have an opportunity to chat together. As I told you, my business structure is very complex and calls go through a switchboard."

"How much does Judson Olney know?" Mason asked.

"Not a thing, not a thing, and I don't want him to know anything."

"But he knows that this whole plant with Della Street is a fake."

"Certainly. He thinks I wanted to introduce Della Street to a certain individual who is here tonight."

"Who?" Mason asked.

"Barrington," Warren said. "You'll find his name on the guest list. Now, this is my bedroom and—"

Mason stepped inside and closed the door. "All

right, Warren," he said, "tell me about Barrington."

"Actually there's nothing to tell," Warren said. "George P. Barrington is the son of Wendell Barrington, the great oil tycoon. George is playing around with some oil properties and I have some properties which can be leased. He's interested in a lease on those properties.

"Confidentially, Mason, I don't give a hang whether he closes the lease or not but I invited him here tonight because he's been going with a trashy young woman who is no good at all. They've split up now. I told Judson Olney that I wanted him to meet Della Street."

"And how does Olney figure that *you* knew Della Street?"

"A couple of weeks ago," Warren said, "I addressed a meeting of the Legal Secretaries Association. I told Olney that Della Street was there, that I hadn't met her but that I had been impressed by her beauty, had found out who she was, and that I would like to have him invite her to come this evening and, of course, bring an escort. I said that I wanted him to be particularly certain she met George Barrington. Now, that's *all* Olney knows.

"Now I've simply got to get back to my guests, Mason. A casual tour of the place is one thing but being away long enough to have a conference with you would be quite another. That would defeat the very purpose of all my planning."

Horace Warren firmly opened the door and

stood waiting for Mason to go through.

"What are *you* afraid of?" Mason asked.

"Me? Nothing. Why?"

"You're afraid to call your soul your own. You're frightened to death of having anyone think you've consulted me. Instead of running your office staff, you're letting the staff run you. Now, what's the answer?"

"Just what I've told you," Warren said hastily. "We have no time for detailed explanations now, Mason."

"When will we have?"

"I don't know. Moreover, it's not important. You know what you have to do. You have a free hand—a blank check. Just protect Lorna."

Mason said, "You're a very remarkable actor, Warren. Tell me about your training."

Warren seemed to relax and expand. "At one time in my life I was stage-struck. I even acted as angel for a couple of shows—but don't let anyone know about that, particularly Lorna. She would think that— Well, you know the general type of thinking that is associated with . . . with things of that sort."

"No, I don't," Mason said. "Shows have to be financed and it's a business proposition."

"I know, I know, but— You're a bachelor, aren't you, Mason?"

"Yes."

"That tells the whole story," Warren said, marching firmly down the corridor and into the big living area where the cocktail party had now been in progress long enough so that the masculine voices were a little louder, the feminine laughter a little more shrill.

"Now, if you don't mind," Warren went on firmly, "I'm going to keep away from you for the rest of the evening."

"Where's Barrington?" Mason asked.

"The man over there who is so busily engaged in talking to your secretary," Warren said.

Mason sized up the tall, slender individual in his early thirties who looked very much like a model of a shirt and collar advertisement; broad-shouldered, slim-waisted, bronzed, high cheekbones, and an air of complete poise.

"I knew he'd fall for Della Street," Warren said. "Look at him, he's fallen hard."

Mason turned to Warren. "Now look here, Warren, I'm not certain I like this. I don't know just what sort of a game you're playing but quite apparently you're trying to use Della Street as bait of some sort for a deal with Barrington."

"No, no," Warren said hastily, "that's just the gambit I used with Judson Olney. But I knew Barrington would fall for her—hard. Now if you'll excuse me, Mason . . ."

Warren turned and walked away.

Mason stood for a moment looking at Barrington, studying the man's quite obvious attempt to impress Della Street.

Then a woman holding a cocktail glass in her left hand swooped down on Perry Mason and demanded to know the magic recipe which he used for winning all his cases. Within a moment she was joined by two more people and Mason found himself a center of attraction.

Chapter Four

PROMPTLY AT ten o'clock Mason rescued Della Street from a group of men who were at no pains to conceal their admiration, said good night to his host and hostess and watched while Judson Olney made quite a production of saying good night, including a kiss on Della Street's right cheek.

"Now that I've found you," he said, "I don't intend to lose you again." And then he added with subtle emphasis, "And I mean every word of this, Della."

Mrs. Warren said, "Having staked out your claim you'd better stay in possession of it, Judson, or someone's going to jump it."

Olney said, "You just watch me."

Mason, turning his head, caught a glance of malevolent hatred directed at Della Street. He knew that the young woman with the blazing eyes was named Chester, and he had heard someone call her Adelle. The lawyer made a mental note to interrogate Della about her when they reached the office.

Horace Warren shook hands with Mason warmly. "We're very much indebted to Judson Olney," he said, "and to Miss Street. Believe me, it was a real treat meeting you, Mr. Mason, and I certainly hope we see more of you."

Mason bowed, thanked him, and with Della Street on his arm left the house. When they came to the place where they had parked the car, he helped Della in and started the motor.

She laughed merrily. "You look like a man who is just getting out of the dentist's chair."

Mason guided the car out of the driveway, said, "I'm bored by small talk, I'm tired of standing up and walking around from group to group, I detest women who deliberately get themselves boiled and then try to simulate owlish sobriety."

"There was only one," Della Street said. "The others were delightful."

"That one was enough," Mason said. "She'd follow me around with a cocktail glass in her left hand, her right forefinger hooking at the lapel of my coat as though she was afraid I was going to get away. . . . Who is the bottled blonde who regarded you as an insect of some sort?"

"That," Della Street said, "was Adelle Chester. George Barrington brought her up and introduced us. She managed to take an instant dislike to me. She wasn't the only one. There was one other woman there, Rosalie Harvey. I don't know whether you noticed her. She was dark-haired with green eyes. She was wearing a—"

46

"I noticed her," Mason interrupted. "Isn't she connected with the business in some way?"

"Judson Olney's secretary," Della said. "She's been with him for five years. I think she smelled a rat and I also think she was bursting with curiosity, but she didn't quite dare ask direct questions."

"Well," Mason said, "it's easy to account for the enmity of these two girls. Barrington was making a great play for you and neglected the girl he was with, so that explains Adelle Chester's attitude. Then after the build-up Olney gave you and told how he had lost his heart to you in the moonlight, it's not difficult to understand the attitude of his devoted secretary who has secretly been idolizing him for years but who never gets a tumble.

"There wasn't any evidence of hostility on the part of anyone else— Just how does Judson Olney fit into the picture?"

"As manager of most of the enterprises, he's Horace Warren's right hand."

"Rather young for such a responsible position, isn't he?"

"It depends on how you look at it. He's smart; believe me, he's smart, and *he* was doing a lot of thinking."

"About what?"

"About you being there."

"Yes," Mason said, "I suppose it would take a lot of doing to palm that off as simply being an accidental circumstance, particularly in view of the fact that I keep my social life sharply limited. What was supposed to be the occasion for the gathering, Della?"

"That," Della said, "I don't know. I assume they do a lot of entertaining, with that house and the setup they have. But this was a conglomerate party. Barrington was invited because of business reasons. Some of the people were from the organization. A couple of them were neighbors. Others, it seems, were members of a bridge club Mrs. Warren belongs to, and that was about it. . . . I gather you didn't have a good time?"

"I earned my five hundred dollars," Mason said. "Don't think I'm an old grouch, Della, but a professional man can seldom enjoy himself at a gathering of that kind. I must have had five different people come to me and start talking in general terms about the law and about my career and then finally get around to bringing up some little legal problem of their own on which they wanted my advice.

"A doctor can seldom attend a social gathering without having people start reciting symptoms and asking him for his opinion."

"Where did you and Horace Warren go after you went out to the swimming pool?" Della asked. "I tried to keep my eye on you but you disappeared somewhere out by the shower."

"We went through a door into a bathroom," Mason said. "Then through the bathroom into Lorna Warren's bedroom."

Della raised her eyebrows.

"Warren wanted to show me a suitcase which he said had forty-seven thousand dollars in it, which his wife was keeping in her closet."

"You saw that suitcase?" she asked.

"I saw the suitcase," Mason said, "but all that was in it at the time we looked were some newspapers."

"Then she'd already paid the blackmail?"

"That's what Warren thinks."

"You don't?"

Mason said, "When a person pays blackmail he turns over the money. If Mrs. Warren had been blackmailed she'd have put the suitcase on the bed, opened the suitcase, taken out the forty-seven thousand dollars, given it to the blackmailer and put the empty suitcase back in the closet.

"When a person takes money out of a suitcase and then stuffs old newspapers into the suitcase to give it approximately the same weight, that looks more like the work of a burglar."

"Good heavens, if someone had stolen forty-seven thousand dollars . . . !" Della Street said, and then let her voice trail off into silence.

"Exactly," Mason said, "but it goes deeper than that. If someone is putting a bite on Mrs. Warren for that amount of money, it's something rather important, and when Mrs. Warren goes to pay him off and opens the suitcase and finds that in place of the money she had left in there, there's nothing but a stack of old newspapers, the fat is apt to be in the fire. You can't pay a blackmailer with a stack of old newspapers."

"I should say not," Della said, and then became silent as she contemplated the picture of what might happen if Mrs. Warren, not knowing the money had disappeared, should open the suitcase.

After a moment she asked, "But who could have taken the money?"

Mason said, "The blackmailer, knowing she had the money in cash waiting to pay him, could have sneaked in, stolen the money, and then, denying he knew anything of the theft, demanded payment."

"That's a thought!" she exclaimed.

"Or," Mason went on, "someone who didn't want her to pay blackmail could have taken the money out of the suitcase and substituted old newspapers."

"Someone who didn't want her to pay blackmail?" she echoed.

"Exactly," Mason said.

"But that could have been the husband!" she exclaimed.

Mason's silence was eloquent.

Della Street, thinking over the various possibilities brought up by this idea, said, "And then, when she went to pay the blackmailer and told him she'd had the money there but had been robbed, he'd call her a liar and . . . and then there *would* be complications . . . and you'd have been retained to protect her, and—Chief, that's what *did* happen! Warren must have removed the money himself."

50

"We can't prove it," Mason said.

After that they were silent until they reached Mason's office.

"I take it that you had a good time," Mason said, as he switched on the office lights.

"I had a *wonderful* time," she told him.

Mason said. "Probably we should have a more active social life. We keep running from one murder case to another like a hummingbird flitting from one—"

"Now, don't compare murders with honey-suckle," she interrupted, "and don't be so grim. This case is just an ordinary blackmail case."

Mason shook his head. "It isn't ordinary, Della, and I'm not even certain it's blackmail."

"Why?"

Mason said, "I have never had a case where the client was at such pains to avoid me."

"What do you mean? Mr. Warren took you around the house, he was talking with you a dozen times during the evening, and—"

"Oh, that," Mason interposed. "That's the preliminary build-up. That's all right, but you notice that Warren has been at great pains to impress upon me that he isn't going to be available, that there's no way I can reach him when I want to without jeopardizing the things he wants to accomplish."

Della Street brought out the coffee percolator, filled it, connected it to the electric socket.

"The Drake Catering Service did quite a job," she said.

"A fine job. That was good champagne, too."

"Do you suppose we'll be invited again to another one?" Della asked.

"I doubt it. Warren wanted to get us familiar with the situation and then keep us at arm's length."

She smiled. "You forget I have my old cruising crush, Judson Olney."

"Yes," Mason said, "you have him. He started out acting under orders from Warren, but I had the feeling that he was putting a lot of enthusiasm into his acting along toward the last."

"A lot of enthusiasm is right," she said. "He wants to find out what it's all about. And speaking of acting, did you know that Horace Warren had always wanted to be an actor, that he still practices in front of a mirror, using a tape recorder?"

Mason settled himself comfortably in a chair, pulled up another chair for his feet, and lit a cigarette. "The trouble with a man of that sort is that he overdoes it," he said. "He becomes too much of a ham. He gets to thinking how good he is and adds just a little too much emotion, a little too much expression, a little too much in the way of gestures."

Drake's knuckles tapped his code knock on the door of Mason's private office.

Della Street let him in.

"Hello, caterer," Mason said. "We didn't expect you so soon."

"I got away early. My share of the work was

done,'' Drake said, then went on with a grin, ''When you become an executive you can leave the dirty dishes for others.''

''They aren't washing those dishes, are they?'' Mason asked.

''Not in that outfit, no. They take them to the main plant to be processed. Every one of those dishes is dried by hand and then they are polished with a towel so that there isn't the faintest sign of a fingerprint on them and every bit of the glass is smooth and clean.''

''The fingerprint crew worked efficiently?''

''Very.''

''All right, what did you find out, Paul?''

''We found out who made the fingerprint you wanted to know about but we didn't find out until right at the last.''

''How come?''

''The fingerprint was made by someone we weren't particularly interested in. We were lifting fingerprints from the other glasses and dishes and only took this one as a last resort.''

''Whose fingerprint was it?'' Mason asked.

Drake said, ''The fingerprint of Mrs. Warren.''

''Lorna Warren, eh?'' Mason said thoughtfully. ''I might have known.''

''How could you possibly have known that?'' Della asked.

''Remember Warren's peculiar attitude and his somewhat peculiar instructions? He said I was to protect his wife from the person who made that fingerprint no matter who the person was and no matter how much it cost. Then he took elaborate precautions to see that we weren't in a position to advise him what we had discovered concerning the fingerprint."

"You mean," Della Street said, "that he's paying a price in order to have you protect his wife from herself?"

Mason nodded, turned to Paul Drake. "Paul, did you get enough fingerprints so you can get a classification?"

"On nearly everyone there," Drake said. "Some of them were smudged but for the most part we managed to get ten reasonably clear fingerprints of everyone there."

"Including Mrs. Warren?"

"I know we got hers."

"All right," Mason said. "Have some police friend get in touch with the FBI. See if she's got a criminal record."

"A *criminal* record!" Drake said. "Are you nuts?"

"I don't think so, Paul. You don't blackmail a person unless you have a club."

"But she's big-time stuff," Drake objected.

"The bigger the quarry, the bigger the club," Mason told him.

"How much time have I got?" Drake asked.

"If you get along with five hours' sleep tonight," Mason said, "you'll have until nine o'clock tomorrow morning our time. That will be noon Washington time."

"That's going to take some awfully fast action

on the part of police and FBI," Drake pointed out, "and I'm going to have to go without a lot of shut-eye tonight in order to get those ten fingerprints collected and classified."

Mason indicated the coffee percolator. "Della Street will see that you have enough coffee to keep you awake, Paul—before I escort her home."

Drake passed over his coffee cup, sighed, and said, "With plenty of cream and sugar, Della, please."

Chapter Five

PAUL DRAKE was in Mason's office at eleven-thirty the following morning.

"Hi, Paul," Mason said. "Any sleep?"

"A surprising amount," Drake said. "I had the fingerprints collected and classified by one-thirty in the morning, a friendly police chief wired the FBI and we have a reply."

"Criminal?" Mason asked.

"Yes and no," Drake said.

"Shoot."

"Mrs. Warren's maiden name was Margaret Lorna Neely. She worked as a secretary for a man named Collister Damon Gideon."

"Where was all this?" Mason asked.

"New York."

"Go ahead."

"Gideon was a promoter; a quick-thinking, fast-talking spellbinder. He had been in trouble with the postal authorities on two previous occasions but they couldn't make any charge stick. The third time they nailed him."

"What charge?" Mason asked.

"Using the mails to defraud. Now, here's the strange thing. They indicted both Gideon and his secretary, Margaret Lorna Neely, and they went to trial in Federal Court.

"I haven't had time to find out too much about that trial but I know the highlights. Gideon was convicted on several counts. The jury acquitted Margaret Neely."

"You know why?" Mason asked.

"Why they convicted Gideon or why they acquitted Margaret Neely?"

"Either."

"They convicted Gideon because he didn't make a good impression. He was too suave and fast-talking, and he'd made the mistake of getting mixed up in a deal where his suckers were farmers. The prosecuting witnesses were the good old horny-handed sons of soil, and the jurors contrasted those honest people with Gideon's smooth line of gab.

"As far as the acquittal is concerned, it's the old story. A fresh face, an innocent manner, a young girl and nylon. Margaret Neely was just twenty-six at the time."

"It seems strange the prosecutor would try them both together," Mason said.

"He did it because he wanted to convict Margaret Neely the worst way."

"Why? Did he think she was criminally responsible?"

"I don't think the evidence that they could

introduce was too clear against her. The main thing that they wanted was forty-seven thousand bucks.''

Mason raised an inquiring eyebrow.

"When the postal inspectors came down like a thousand bricks and the authorities moved in, they found Gideon with virtually empty pockets, an empty safe and an empty bank account. He had, however, in some mysterious manner arranged to pay attorneys' fees in advance and there had been a checking account with a balance of some forty-seven thousand dollars which mysteriously vanished.''

"Doesn't the bank have records?" Mason asked.

"Oh, sure. Gideon drew the money out. He said he put it in the office safe because he knew some disgruntled customers were going to call on him the next day and he had intended to make restitution in hard cash because he didn't want to have any paper records of the transaction.''

"And the safe, I take it, was conveniently burglarized during the night.''

"The safe was conveniently burglarized during the night.''

"And I also take it the authorities never found the forty-seven thousand dollars.''

"That's right. And there was just a whisper of suspicion that Margaret Neely knew where the money was and may have been saving it for Collister Gideon, as salvage from the wrecking operation the government did on the business.

"Incidentally, the police would like very, very much indeed—and the FBI would like very, very much indeed—to know where Margaret Neely is now and where I picked up her fingerprints. A great deal of pressure is being brought to bear on me."

"All right," Mason said. "You can't say anything."

"Well, it's quite a bit of pressure," Drake protested. "They're even intimating that I might be aiding and abetting a criminal."

"Criminal nothing," Mason said. "Margaret Neely was acquitted of any crime in connection with the fraud."

"Well, she did a good job of vanishing," Drake said. "Police thought they were going to be able to keep in touch with her through social security numbers or something of that sort, but Margaret Neely just simply vanished. From what *we* know, we can put two and two together. She must have met Horace Warren soon after that. She was then going under the name of Lorna Neely and evidently had gone to Mexico City.

"In those days Warren was a struggling young businessman with lots of ambition and a reasonable amount of property. He hadn't hit the jackpot as yet. That came two years later when he struck oil on some of his property and from then on he made shrewd investments."

Mason grinned. "You've been gossiping, Paul."

"I've been listening."

"No one has any idea where you got these fingerprints?"

"I won't say that," Drake said. "No one knows anything from me, but it's possible I may have left a back trail."

"How come?"

"Getting that fingerprint catering service last night."

Mason was thoughtful. "I see, Paul. . . . Even so, I should think the authorities would be willing to live and let live. They put Margaret Neely on trial and she was acquitted. What more do they want!"

"They're after Collister Gideon."

"They got him."

"They got the empty shell," Drake said. "They intimated that if Gideon wanted to cough up the forty-seven thousand bucks he could get parole and a chance to be released."

"Gideon refused?"

"Gideon insisted he has absolutely no knowledge of the money. He insisted the safe was burglarized during the night."

"He claimed it was an inside job?"

"No, he claimed very vehemently it was an outside job. The combination to the safe was pasted on the bottom side of the drawer in his desk. The authorities found that the drawer had been pulled out of the desk, the contents dumped on the floor, and burglars had evidently secured the combination to the safe, opened it and taken out the money."

"Any other evidence that the office had been burglarized?"

"Quite a bit, as I understand it. The lock on the door had been tampered with. About twenty dollars that Margaret Neely kept in her desk was missing, and the money from the petty cash drawer, amounting to about ninety-seven dollars, was gone and even the money from the stamp drawer, all of the dimes and pennies that had been put in by persons taking out stamps for personal correspondence."

"So Gideon wouldn't make a deal and take parole?"

"He said he couldn't. He said he didn't know anything about the money."

"How long's he in for?" Mason asked.

"He was released last Friday," Drake said.

Mason was thoughtful. "And I suppose the authorities have had shadows sticking to him like glue."

"That I wouldn't know about," Drake said, "but I can tell you this. It's one hell of a job to keep a man under surveillance when he knows what the score is and doesn't want to be shadowed. He can break away sooner or later.

"The best technique is to let him make a first try and encourage him to believe that he's thrown off the shadows and then see what he does. For that reason authorities quite frequently have a rough shadow who keeps the guy under surveillance in such a way that the shadow stands out like a sore thumb. Then the subject ditches the shadow by going into a crowded building which has several exits, or getting a car, driving through a traffic light or two just as it's changing, and all the familiar dodges. The rough shadow gets left behind and the smooth shadows take over.

"Usually the subject will go and hole up somewhere in a little hotel under an assumed name and keep completely quiet for a couple of days. Then if he sees nothing suspicious, he thinks he has it made and goes out and walks right into the trap."

"Did this happen with Gideon?"

"I don't know anything about Gideon," Drake said. "The authorities aren't taking me into their confidence except to tell me that I'd better cooperate or else."

Drake drew an extended forefinger across his throat.

"You sit tight," Mason said. "If it comes to an absolute showdown where they threaten you with your license, you can tell them that I gave you the fingerprints and that you reported to me. Let them talk with me and I'll tell them."

"Well," Drake said, "they'd still like the forty-seven thousand bucks."

"So they could make restitution?" Mason asked.

"Well, they would like to nail Gideon again because of giving false information to officers."

"That's all been outlawed by the statute of limitations a long time ago," Mason said.

"No, it hasn't," Drake said. "They played it

62

smarter than that. They pulled out Gideon's statements about the office safe having been burglarized and so forth and told him they were investigating that crime. Gideon told them it had all been outlawed by the statute of limitations but they told him they were investigating it anyway and asked him again to tell them about the burglary of the office and the loss of the forty-seven thousand dollars.

"They have some sort of a statute about giving false information to officers who are investigating a crime and—"

Mason made an exclamation of annoyance. "Gideon has served his time. He's paid his debt to society."

"But they don't like to have a crook get away with forty-seven thousand dollars and only serve a few years."

"I see," Mason said thoughtfully. "Well, the police know that you know something about Margaret Neely. You're going to have to handle the connection so all they have is a blind alley."

"I'm terminating the connection," Drake said. "I don't want any part of it. I'm washing my hands of the whole business."

Mason shook his head. "No you aren't."

"What do you mean by that, Perry? I have my license at stake. I can't hold out information the police want in the investigation of a crime."

Mason said, "The police aren't going to prosecute anyone for anything. They'd like to impound forty-seven thousand dollars. That's all.

I'd let you off the hook and get another detective agency if I could, but I don't dare contact anyone else.

"Think what a mess would be stirred up if it became known Lorna Warren had been arrested! We can't let that happen. We can't let that information get out."

"No one's letting it out," Drake said.

Mason was openly doubtful. "When the police get mad, Paul, their methods are sometimes pretty rough."

Drake said nothing.

Mason said, "I want shadows, Paul. I want Mrs. Warren kept under discreet surveillance. Don't let her get on to the fact she's being shadowed. Tell your men to let her get away rather than arouse her suspicions.

"I also want Judson Olney tagged for a few days at least, and I want you to get a mug shot of Collister Gideon and see that all your operatives study the picture. If either of the people I've mentioned sees him, or if he gets in touch with them, I want to know about it."

Drake groaned. "I was afraid you'd have some idea like this. It's dangerous, Perry."

"Taking a bath is dangerous, Paul. Get started."

When Drake had left the office Della Street said, "Good heavens! You'd think she'd have had more sense."

Mason said, "Look at it this way. An impressionable young woman, she was completely hypnotized by an older man's glib talk. She thought there was nothing wrong in what they were doing. She was fascinated by him, probably in love. It would have been relatively easy for Gideon to have got her to take custody of the forty-seven thousand bucks."

"I know," Della Street said. "That part is all right, but she certainly shouldn't let a misguided sense of loyalty to a clever crook trap her into the present situation."

"Just what is the present situation?" Mason asked.

"Well," she said, "for one thing, her husband knows."

"Knows what?"

"About the forty-seven thousand dollars."

Mason said, "The chain of circumstantial evidence has some very significant missing links, Della. In the first place, the authorities don't know that Mrs. Horace Warren is Margaret Lorna Neely. In the second place, the husband doesn't know anything about her past, and in the third place, even if the authorities should question her husband, he couldn't be interrogated as a witness because a husband can't testify against a wife, and she can't be forced to testify against herself."

"All right," she said, "how about you? An attorney has to hold the communications of his client privileged, but that doesn't mean he can be inveigled into becoming an accessory to a crime."

"A crime?" Mason asked.

"A crime," she said. "Gideon was convicted. You can't conceal knowledge of a crime."

"And what do I really *know?*" Mason asked. "What knowledge do I have?"

"You know about . . . about . . ."

Mason grinned. "Exactly, Della. I perhaps have some hearsay evidence but all I ever actually *saw* was a suitcase filled with old newspapers. It's no crime to collect newspapers in a suitcase."

"And just where do we go from here?" she asked.

Mason said, "We have been retained to protect Mrs. Horace Warren against the person whose fingerprint was given to us. That print was made by Margaret Lorna Neely. We are, therefore, retained to protect Mrs. Warren from herself."

"You're going to take the assignment literally?"

"There isn't any other way to take it," Mason said. "We're going to protect Mrs. Horace Warren from herself."

"Her past?"

"Her past, her present, everything."

"How can you do that?" she asked. "Mrs. Warren has already turned over the money."

"That doesn't mean Gideon has received the money," Mason said. "Let us assume that it is in transit.

"Horace Warren says the money was still in the suitcase up to a short time before he tried to show it to me. When we opened the suitcase newspapers had been substituted for the currency.

66

"Police would have been following Collister Gideon. He would have anticipated that. Therefore he would hardly have been so foolish as to go directly to the Warren residence and pick up the money. Therefore he must have sent some intermediary."

"Some person who was present at the party?" Della Street asked.

"We can't tell," Mason said. "It may have been one of the servants. Gideon is smart. He knew in advance the date of his release. It is well within the limits of probability that he could have planted an accomplice as a servant."

"Then Mrs. Warren paid over the money?"

"Or the servant stole it," Mason said. "Or the husband stole it so his wife wouldn't be paying blackmail, and then retained me to protect her from the blackmailer."

"What a mess!" Della Street exclaimed.

"But," Mason pointed out, "we have one advantage. We have the fingerprints of everyone who was at that party. By the time the people in that fingerprint van get done classifying them, we can find if anyone there has a criminal record. We'll check on the servants first."

"And suppose we find the thief?" Della Street asked. "Then what? Who makes the complaint?"

Mason grinned. "No one."

"You mean you let the thief get away with forty-seven thousand dollars?"

"I didn't say that," Mason said. "We do a little cloak-and-dagger stuff of our own. Once we've found the thief, we steal the money back again.''

"Couldn't you make a complaint and—"

Mason interrupted with a firm shake of his head. "You can't make a complaint in a situation of that sort—not with the income tax being what it is. Everyone would jump to the conclusion that the forty-seven thousand dollars represented money the Warrens were trying to conceal from their bank account, and therefore were keeping it stored in a suitcase in Mrs. Warren's closet.

"The Bureau of Internal Revenue would move in and want to examine everyone in connection with the case. They'd have to know that the money was being saved to pay some sort of a blackmail demand. They'd look Mrs. Warren up, inquire into her past, and in no time at all would find out about the skeleton in her closet.

"No, Della, the thing has to be handled very circumspectly, and completely under cover."

"And that's why Mrs. Warren has said nothing about the loss of the money?"

"What *could* she say?" Mason asked. "What would *you* say?"

Della Street was thoughtfully silent for a moment, then said, "Nothing, I guess, but it must be horribly frustrating to have forty-seven thousand dollars which has been carefully saved in cash disappear and not be able to utter even a word of protest."

"I think," Mason said, "that describes it very accurately—a horribly frustrating experience."

Chapter Six

LATER THAT afternoon the telephone on Della Street's desk rang a routine summons. Della picked up the receiver, said, "Yes, Gertie," then suddenly her jaw sagged, her eyes grew large, and she said, "Why—Wait— Hold the phone a minute, Gertie."

Della Street turned to Perry Mason. "A man in the office says he is Collister D. Gideon."

"Well, what do you know," Mason said. "I guess we're going to have to give Mr. Gideon credit for being a pretty clever individual. By all means, Della, tell him to come in."

"But Chief, he— Good heavens, that means he must know . . ."

"Know what?"

"Everything."

Mason said. "If he gave Lorna Warren forty-seven thousand dollars to keep for him, he certainly knows about her present whereabouts. If he didn't give her the money to keep for him, but regarded her as a loyal employee, he has probably kept up with what has been happening in her life and that complicates the problem."

"But what can you do?" Della asked. "If he shows up here . . ."

"He *has* shown up here," Mason said, "and that means he thinks he holds the high hand and is going to call for a showdown. I'm becoming very much interested in Collister Damon Gideon. Show the gentleman in, Della. Then tip Gertie to call Paul Drake and have a shadow put on Gideon as soon as he leaves the office."

Della Street said, "I'll be right out, Gertie," hung up the phone, vanished to the outer office and a few moments later returned leading a slim-waisted, well-dressed smiling individual in his late forties into the office.

"This is Mr. Mason," she said.

Gideon didn't offer to shake hands.

"How do you do, Mr. Mason," he said. "I don't know how much you know about me, but I am assuming you know a great deal. May I be seated?"

"By all means," Mason said. "What makes you think I know anything about you?"

"Putting two and two together."

"Would you mind telling me which two and two you put together?" Mason asked.

"Not at all," Gideon said, settling back in the chair, looking around the office with the swift survey of a man who has been forced by environment to make instantaneous and accurate appraisal of his surroundings.

"You see, Mr. Mason," he said calmly, "I'm a crook."

"Indeed," Mason said.

"That is," Gideon amended. "The government says I'm a crook, and a jury of my peers agreed with the government."

"And the aftermath?" Mason asked.

"A term in a federal prison with very little time off."

Mason shook his head with what might have been a gesture of sympathy.

"Now then," Gideon said, "at the time I was in business and ran head on into the governmental forces of so-called righteousness, I had working for me a very beautiful young woman, a Margaret Lorna Neely."

"I take it she wasn't involved," Mason said.

Gideon smiled. "The government tried to involve her but the charges didn't stick. The jury acquitted her and convicted me. The government tried us together, possibly with malice aforethought, feeling that a jury acting on rather weak evidence would salve its conscience by acquitting one defendant and convicting the other."

"You don't seem to be bitter about it," Mason said.

"I don't *seem* to be bitter about it," Gideon said. "It would do very little good to be bitter about it, and the last few years of my life have taught me a great deal, Mr. Mason. One of the things I have learned is not to do things which can't result in any ultimate benefit to me."

"Indeed," Mason said.

"Among other things, those years have taught me that the world, beneath its veneer of civilization, is geared to the ancient principle of survival of the fittest, and in the battle for survival the person who is utterly ruthless has a very decided advantage over the person who practices the so-called Golden Rule."

"I see," Mason said. "You still haven't told me why you came here."

"It pays to read the newspapers," Gideon said, "particularly the society column, and I notice in the afternoon paper that at an informal gathering given by Horace Warren, the noted financier and progressive businessman, the guests were thrilled by the presence of Mr. Perry Mason and his beautiful secretary, Miss Della Street."

Gideon made a slight bow in the direction of Della Street.

"The newspaper account," Gideon went on, "which you may have missed, Mr. Mason, mentioned that the noted attorney was so busy with his law practice that he seldom had time for any social life and the guests lionized him."

"Indeed," Mason said. "I hadn't read the account."

"It was a very interesting account," Gideon said. "Now, in view of the fact that Margaret Lorna Neely is the present Mrs. Horace Warren, and in view of the fact that you seldom attend social gatherings, and in further view of the fact that both you and your secretary were there, I gathered that there was some official reason for your attendance.

"Furthermore, being something of an egotist, I assumed that it was barely possible my release from prison had something to do with the reason you were there.

"Now, if Mrs. Warren had wanted to consult you, she would have gone to your office. If Mr. Warren had wanted to consult you, he might not have cared to call on you at the office. The fact that you were there at his house as a guest would indicate that you had been retained to size up the situation more or less surreptitiously, so to speak."

"In my profession," Mason said, "I have always found that reasoning from a premise may be fallacious and is almost certain to lead to erroneous conclusions."

"Isn't that the truth!" Gideon exclaimed. "You know, I've been betrayed by mistakes of that sort so that I've learned not to make them. However, let's get back to the matter in hand, Mr. Mason."

"In what way?" Mason asked.

"The authorities have been very anxious to locate Margaret Lorna Neely. They seemed to think that I knew where she was.

"Of course, all my correspondence for the last few years has been rigorously censored and I have had to keep in the background. I didn't dare write anyone, nor did I care to have anyone write me. However, I have managed to keep certain bits of information locked up in my head where they couldn't be pried out by inquisitive government officials.

"Would you believe it, Mr. Mason, the government has actually intimated that shortly before my arrest I managed to get some forty-seven thousand dollars in cash and conceal it somewhere so it would be available on my release. They felt perhaps that my co-defendant, Margaret Lorna Neely, might have been selected as the person to keep this money for me, or perhaps half of this sum of money. I don't suppose you would realize it, living in a position of social and financial security, Mr. Mason, but at times government investigators can become very arbitrary, very insulting, and very arrogant."

"I hadn't noticed it," Mason said.

"I didn't think you would have, because, after all, Mr. Mason, the tactics which a government investigator would use with you are somewhat different from the tactics which a government investigator would use with a person convicted of conspiracy to use the mails to defraud."

"The charge was conspiracy?" Mason asked.

"That was one of the charges. They had five counts. The jury acquitted me on three, just in order to make it appear they were impartial and fair, and convicted me on two.

"The principal charge was conspiracy because in that way they were able to drag my secretary into court and smear her reputation with all that publicity. Thank heavens she was able to disappear in such a manner that they lost track of her entirely."

"She must have been very clever to have engineered such a disappearance," Mason said.

"She is very clever."

"And perhaps she had clever friends," Mason ventured.

"That is always a possibility," Gideon admitted. "Do you mind if I smoke?"

"Not at all."

Gideon waved back the cigarettes which Mason extended toward him, took a long slender cigar from his pocket, lit it, got it burning to suit him, then settled back in the chair and smiled affably at Mason. The aroma suggested the cigar was expensive.

"With your legal mind," Gideon said, "you doubtless know why I am here."

"I would prefer to have you tell me," Mason said.

"That's going to be rather crude."

"Miss Street and I have encountered crude approaches before," Mason said.

"I know, but a crude approach is so dreadfully inartistic."

"The approach so far seems to have been rather artistic," Mason said. "So it all may average up."

Gideon sighed. "Well, if I have to get down to brass tacks, I will. You see, the government finally released me after they had held me in prison for every minute of every day that they could legally hold me."

Mason, watching the man, said nothing.

"Immediately after my conviction," Gideon said, "I was told that if I produced the forty-seven thousand dollars the sentence would be much lighter. Then after I was sentenced I was told that if I produced the forty-seven thousand dollars I would stand a very good chance of getting parole."

"You accepted none of these offers?" Mason asked.

"None of them."

"Why?"

"Because," Gideon said, "I had no idea where the forty-seven thousand dollars was. I couldn't have produced it if I had wanted to."

"Now that you have been released," Mason said, "I take it that the interest of the government has ceased."

"Are you kidding?" Gideon asked. "Now that I have been released, the government blood-hounds are baying on my trail hoping that I'll lead them to the money, whereupon they'll pounce upon it and have the last laugh. They'll say, in effect, 'You can't beat the law, Gideon. You served a lot of extra time in prison so you could enjoy that forty-seven thousand dollars when you got out. Now then, *we've* got the money and *you've* served the time. Ha-ha-ha!'

"And of course they'll see that every prison inmate knows all about it and gloat over the fact that you can't beat the law and that they made a sucker out of me."

"So they are following you?" Mason asked.

"Oh, yes."

"They followed you here?" Mason asked.

"Of course."

"I see," Mason said, frowning.

"I can see that you do," Gideon said, smiling. "I'm trying to make an artistic approach on this, Mr. Mason, even if the main gambit will have to be rather crude.

"You see, the government feels that in dealing with a crook it is dealing with a person of very inferior intelligence. When the government does a shadow job on a crook, it is at times very naïve.

"In my case, for instance, they have a rough shadow on my trail."

"A rough shadow?" Mason asked.

"Surely, with your experience in criminal law, you understand the function of a rough shadow," Gideon said. "A rough shadow is just what the name implies. It's a shadow who is so obvious a person simply can't miss him.

"If you'd have your secretary step to the corridor door and open it, I dare say you'd find the rough shadow standing at the corner of the corridor. When the door opened he would very ostentatiously show his embarrassment. Then he would turn and walk along the corridor, peering at the names and numbers on the doors as though looking for some office he was having difficulty finding."

"That's the rough shadow?" Mason asked.

"That's the rough shadow."

"I would assume that the government expected

to accomplish very little by such crude tactics."

"The government expects to accomplish a lot," Gideon said. "The rough shadow is always very ostentatious but rather inept. It is no job at all for a clever man to elude his surveillance. Even a simple thing like driving through a traffic signal just as it is changing would shake the rough shadow."

Gideon stopped talking, watched Mason's face through a blue haze of cigar smoke. His half-closed eyes studied the lawyer thoughtfully.

After a moment he went on. "That, of course, is when the smooth shadow takes over. The smooth shadows are in the background. I don't see them. At least, I'm not supposed to. Having ditched the rough shadow, I will be flushed with confidence and go to a little motel somewhere, register under an assumed name; then get up in the dead of night, move to some other motel; then perhaps into a rooming house, and then, convinced that the government is no longer in touch with me, I'll go and dig up the forty-seven thousand dollars. At least, that's what the government thinks."

"And then they'll pounce on you?"

"Then they'll pounce on me. The smooth shadows will have been keeping up with me all the time."

"Can't you ditch them?" Mason asked.

"Oh, it can be done," Gideon said. "It's not a simple matter but there are ways. It takes time, however, and a certain amount of capital.

"Now, very frankly, Mr. Mason, I have time but I don't have much capital."

"I see," Mason said.

"I thought you could remedy that."

"In what way?"

"I felt that Mr. Horace Warren would be glad to make some contribution toward my rehabilitation."

"You assume Mr. Warren is my client?"

"I assume he is a friend, otherwise you would not have been at his house last night. I also assume your presence at that little gathering was not without some significance. I feel that you have some official contact with someone who is interested. But I see no reason to cudgel my brains over a point which, as far as I'm concerned, is immaterial. The point is that Mr. Warren would follow any suggestion you might make which had for its purpose seeing that his wife's past was not brought into the pitiless glare of publicity."

"And you are threatening to—"

Gideon held up his hand. "No, no, *please,* Mr. Mason. *Please!*"

"I must have misunderstood you then," Mason said.

"You certainly did. The point is this, Mr. Mason. Every move that I make is being reported to the governmental agencies. The fact that I am here this afternoon is causing a lot of speculation. Why did I come here? What possible connection can I have with you or you with me? My correspondence has been censored for years. I've had no contact with you. You haven't written me and I haven't written you.

"Therefore the authorities will assume that you must be representing the person who has the forty-seven thousand dollars and that I am calling on you to try and make a deal."

"I see," Mason said.

"So the government will start checking on your clients, particularly those who have been in touch with you or with whom you have been in touch during the past few days, or with whom you will be in touch after I leave this office.

"You'll be surprised at how efficient some of these government operatives are. They can put two and two together just as I have. They doubtless have read or will read the society column in the evening paper."

"And so?" Mason asked.

"And so they'll wonder why it happens you broke your usual rule to attend what was seemingly a purely social gathering. They'll start probing into the background of the guests, and eventually, of the host and hostess.

"That would be very unfortunate, Mr. Mason."

The lawyer remained silent.

"Now then," Gideon said, "if Mr. Warren would make a contribution toward my financial welfare, it would give me the margin I need to ditch the government's smooth shadows, vanish completely and be on my way."

"Otherwise?" Mason asked.

"Otherwise," Gideon said, "I am trapped in an economic net. They stripped me clean when they sent me to prison. They released me with only what is referred to as 'gate money.' "

Mason regarded the man's clothes and the cigar. "You seem to have done very well for yourself in a short period of time."

Gideon smiled. "Let us say," he said, "that I am resourceful and not entirely unintelligent."

"And so you come to me?" Mason asked.

"And so I come to you," Gideon said.

"And if your requests are not complied with?"

"Then I keep coming to you," Gideon said. "Every time I come to you it causes more and more speculation on the part of the government. And if, after my visits, you get in touch with Horace Warren or his wife, that triggers an investigation which would be disastrous to the welfare of your clients."

"This is a very interesting form of blackmail," Mason said.

"Please, *please,* Mr. Mason! *Don't use that word!* This is not blackmail. I have the greatest respect for Horace Warren and I am very, very fond of his wife. I wish them every happiness. I am trying to give them an opportunity to achieve that happiness.

"If I remain financially embarrassed, it is almost certain that sooner or later I will have to betray myself. Some clue will crop up which will enable the authorities to know the real identity of Lorna Warren. Of course, they don't

81

have anything against her at the moment, but they would bring her in and question her and it would soon become known that she was none other than Margaret Lorna Neely who was tried and acquitted for conspiracy to defraud by use of the mails.

"Now surely, Mr. Mason, you wouldn't want that to happen, and Mr. Warren, with his present social and business contacts, wouldn't want it to happen.

"I don't want any financial consideration given me to keep quiet. That *would* be blackmail. I simply want to vanish. I want to elude the smooth shadows of the government. In order to do that I need money. I have to be able to buy an automobile."

"Why an automobile?" Mason asked.

"Because I would need that in order to ditch the smooth shadows and disappear."

"Surely," Mason said, "the government operatives could follow an automobile."

"Oh, of course. That's the simplest thing in the world, particularly in these days when they have electronic shadowing devices. They simply put a little installation on my automobile and the thing gives off little 'beeps' which would enable government detectives in an automobile to follow me without the slightest bit of trouble. They wouldn't even need to get close to me. They could get three or four blocks behind me and still have no difficulty following me."

"Then perhaps you'd better explain why you

want the automobile," Mason said.

"I would want to play the same trick on the government detectives that they are trying to play on me. In other words, they want me to become overconfident and I want them to become overconfident.

"You see, Mr. Mason, I wouldn't get a new car, and I would buy it on a contract. Then I would assume the initiative. It has been my experience that one can do very much better when he has the initiative.

"Of course, the money with which I paid for the automobile would be pounced upon by government agents who would look it over for some clue. I would, therefore, like to have this money in older bills of five- and ten-dollar denominations and some ones. It would appear that I had put the bite on someone who had had to dig deep into his savings in order to get that money."

"Go on," Mason said.

"Then," Gideon went on, "I would take that automobile and let the government think that I had no idea there were any smooth shadows on the job. I'd ditch the rough shadow, which, as I said, wouldn't be very much of a job."

"Go on," Mason said.

"So then the smooth shadows would handle things in such a way that they would flatter themselves that I would have no idea I was being shadowed. They might perhaps have as many as five cars on the job. They might even work with a helicopter and binoculars."

"And they'd keep you in sight?" Mason asked.

Gideon grinned and said, "Of course."

"They could do that?" Mason asked.

"They're clever," Gideon said, "and they hold all the face cards. I would, of course, go through all the expected motions. I'd take a lot of evasive tactics so the government detectives would know that I felt certain I had ditched the rough shadow. I would then go into a restaurant to eat, and leave the car parked outside.

"While I was eating, the government agents would, of course, put an electronic bug on the car so that I would be shadowed by cars that were two or three blocks away."

"Just how would you handle that situation?" Mason asked.

Gideon smiled. "You have to leave me with some cards I don't turn face up, Mr. Mason. I'd handle it. The government agents would never see me again. Just when they were flushed with triumph, I'd trump their aces and be on my way."

"You're certain you could do that?" Mason asked.

"I'm certain."

"The government has some good men who are highly trained," Mason said.

Gideon's silence was eloquent.

"In other words," Mason said, "if you get this money I'll never see you again?"

"Exactly."

"And if you don't get it?"

"I'll be in daily touch with you."

"You realize that after this initial experience I wouldn't ever see you again," Mason said. "I'd let you cool your heels in the outer office until you got tired."

"No," Gideon said, puffing at the cigar, then removing it from his mouth and turning it so he could inspect the burning tobacco, "I rather think you'd see me, Mr. Mason. I think you'd be instructed to see me."

"And do what?"

"Give me money."

"How much money?"

Gideon moved his hands in an expansive gesture. "You would, of course, want me to make a good job of it. You wouldn't want me to play right into their hands. You'd want to be sure that I didn't come back, because of course once I ditched the smooth shadows they'd put a stake-out on your office."

"And would probably assume that I had given you the money with which to purchase an automobile."

"They might."

"And might even question me."

"Oh, I think you can count on that," Gideon said. "I think they'd be certain to question you. After they once woke up to the fact that they had been outwitted, they'd be rather annoyed. They'd question you. They'd think perhaps you had thought up the scheme for outwitting them. They'd talk about compounding felonies, about being an accessory after the fact; they'd be rather rough. But I'm assuming that you would simply sit back in your chair, with an enigmatic smile, and tell them that if they thought they had any case against you, to go right ahead and prosecute you; otherwise, to just keep the hell out of your office and leave you alone."

"All of this has been most entertaining," Mason said, "but it just happens, Gideon, that I don't know anyone who would be likely to give you any sum of money."

"You know the Warrens."

"I don't know them well enough to go to them and suggest that they should pay blackm—"

Once more Gideon held up his hand. "Please, Mr. Mason, *please* don't use that word. It has unsavory connotations and it bothers me. It's crude."

"What do you think this is that you're doing?" Mason asked.

"I'm simply putting cards on the table."

"You're asking for money in return for silence."

"No, I'm not. I'm suggesting that perhaps you might care to communicate with people who would like to see that I had money for my rehabilitation."

"And in the event you don't get the money, you're making threats."

"No, no! No threats," Gideon said. "After all, Mr. Mason, I haven't threatened you."

"You've said that you would keep coming back here."

"I'm rather persistent," Gideon said. "After all, there's no law which says I can't come to your office as often as I like. It's a public place. I am acting on the assumption that you will either advise some of your clients or, let us say, some of your friends, to pay me some money to see that I don't keep hanging around or that you will be instructed by those people to see that I get enough money so I can get out.

"Well, I mustn't detain you, Mr. Mason. You're a busy man, a *very* busy man."

Gideon got to his feet.

Mason said, "Don't ever try to put pressure on me, Gideon. We deal with lots of blackmailers in this business. If I thought you were resorting to blackmail, I'd deal with you accordingly."

"And how is that?" Gideon asked, smiling ominously as he stood in the exit doorway.

"We have various methods of dealing with blackmailers," Mason said.

"I dare say you do," Gideon said. "And I certainly wouldn't want you to put me in that category. However, I would like to know, just as a matter of curiosity, how you *do* deal with blackmailers."

"There are three methods," Mason said.

"Indeed?"

"One," Mason said, holding up his right index finger, "you pay off."

"Very sensible," Gideon said.

87

"Two," Mason went on holding up a second finger, "you confide in the police. They protect your secret. You catch the blackmailer red-handed and he goes to prison."

"Very nice *if* it works," Gideon said. "Now, what's the third method?"

Mason met his eyes, held up a third finger. "The third method," he said, "is that you kill the son of a bitch."

For a moment Gideon recoiled. "You can't go to the police, and I can hardly fancy you as a murderer, Mr. Mason."

"Guess again," Mason said. "You, yourself, said that the utterly ruthless person had all the advantage in this world."

"Well," Gideon said, "since I am not a blackmailer, the discussion is simply academic. I will, however, be in touch with you from time to time, Mr. Mason, and I feel certain you will become interested in, shall we say, my rehabilitation?"

He bowed from the waist.

"Thank you for seeing me, Mr. Mason." He turned, again bowed from the waist. "Miss Street," he said, his eyes and voice appreciative.

Then he opened the exit door and walked out into the corridor without once looking back.

Della Street looked at Perry Mason in dismay. "Why did you say that about killing him?"

"I'll give *him* something to think about," Mason said.

"Shall I try to get hold of Mr. Warren?" she asked.

"Heavens, no," Mason said. "Remember that Warren told me calls had to go through his switchboard, that it would be very difficult to get hold of him, and that our conversations would be restricted."

"You mean you aren't going to let him know anything about *this* conversation?"

"Exactly," Mason said. "He paid me to handle the situation and I'll handle it."

Chapter Seven

IT WAS shortly before five o'clock that the telephone rang and Della Street, picking up the instrument, said, "Yes, Gertie," then suddenly puckered her face in a frown. "You know I don't take personal calls here, Gertie— Just a minute."

Della Street put her palm over the transmitter, turned to Mason and said, "Some woman who refuses to give her name states that she wants to talk with me about Judson Olney. What do I do?"

Mason picked up his own telephone, said, "Gertie, put me in on Della Street's call but don't say anything about my being on the line."

"Okay, Gertie," Della Street said, "I'll take the call."

Mason, listening in, heard a feminine voice, harsh with emotion. "Look here, Miss Della Street, I want to know what you think you're trying to get away with. For your information, I looked up the passenger list on the *Queen of Jamaica* at the time Judson Olney made the trip,

90

and you weren't listed as a passenger. I thought the whole thing was phony when I first heard the story.

"Now, I want to know just what you're trying to pull.

"Don't think you can get away with any fast one as far as *my* man is concerned. I'm the kind to fight, and when I fight I fight dirty. Now, will you kindly tell me just what this is all about?"

Mason motioned to Della Street to hang up the phone, and then hung up simultaneously with her.

"Well," Della Street said, "that's another complication. Good heavens, Chief, she was certainly boiling mad."

Mason said, "That's the trouble with letting an amateur write a script and then trying to act it out. Who do you suppose that was, Della?"

"I would say it was either Rosalie Harvey or Adelle Chester. I couldn't recognize the voice."

Mason said, "Well, the fat's in the fire. Someone went to the trouble to check on the passenger list when Olney made that cruise. Amateur liars are always amateurish, Della. We let them write the script. We shouldn't have done it."

"Now we're in a spot where . . ."

Gertie, the receptionist, appeared in the doorway to the inner office. "A Mr. George P. Barrington is waiting to see you, Mr. Mason. He says he has to see you on a matter of the greatest importance and I think he's all worked up about something.

"He said to tell you that he met you at Mr. Warren's."

Mason exchanged glances with Della Street.

"I came in personally," she said, "because he's trying to pump me."

"In what way?" Mason asked.

"He's asking me about Della Street, about where she goes on her vacations, and if I remember the time she went to the Caribbean."

Mason said to Della Street, "Go in the law library, Della. Go out through the door from the law library and go home. I'll talk with Barrington alone. I think perhaps he said he was calling to see me but he actually wants to talk with you. If he wants to talk with you it'll be about that confounded Caribbean cruise. . . . Why in hell can't clients be better liars?"

"He's nice," Della Street said.

"He may be nice," Mason pointed out, "but he fell for you like a ton of bricks and he had a young woman with him who seemed to be bored with it all but who was seething inside. She's probably told him you never were on that cruise with Judson Olney."

Mason said to Gertie, "Keep him waiting about thirty seconds, Gertie. Don't let him inveigle you into conversation about anything or anybody. As soon as Della gets out through the law library, I'll give the phone a jiggle and you can send him in."

"Yes, Mr. Mason," Gertie said, her eyes big and round, looking from one to the other. Then, rather reluctantly, she left for the outer office.

"Now you've done it," Della Street said. "Gertie loves mysteries. She likes to take a button and sew a vest on it. She'll work out some deep, dark intrigue that—"

Mason motioned toward the law library. "On your way," he said. "I'm going to tell Mr. Barrington you've gone home for the evening, and when I tell a lie I like to have it the truth."

"On my way," Della Street said, grabbing her purse, pausing for a swift look in the mirror, then vanishing through the door to the law library.

Mason waited a few seconds, then picked up the telephone and said, "Okay, Gertie."

A moment later George P. Barrington came hurrying into the office.

"Hello, Mr. Mason," he said. "Nice of you to see me without an appointment. I am a little concerned about something that happened this afternoon."

"Yes?" Mason asked.

"Your secretary, is she here?"

"She's left for the day," Mason said.

"I received an anonymous telephone call that bothered me a lot."

"Who called?" Mason asked.

"I don't know."

"Man or woman?"

"I can't even tell you that for sure, but I think it was a woman trying to make her voice deep and . . . well, disguised."

"Recognize who was talking from the spacing

of the words, or any little trick of expression?" Mason asked.

"No. . . . Why?"

"I was just wondering," Mason said. "What was the purpose of the call?"

"The purpose of the call was to tell me that your presence at the gathering last night was in a purely professional capacity, that Horace Warren had arranged for you to be there to keep an eye on me, that Judson Olney hadn't been on any boat trip with Della Street and hadn't known her until a short time prior to that party."

"Well," Mason said, "that's very considerate of the young woman, isn't it? And just why would I be retained to keep an eye on you?"

"That was what I hoped you would tell *me*," Barrington said.

"I can't tell you something I don't know, and I can't waste my time answering anonymous telephone accusations."

"I hoped that you would say that my informant was entirely in error, that you were there purely in a social capacity, and that Miss Street did know Judson Olney and had known him for some time."

"And that would have relieved your mind?" Mason said.

"Frankly, it would."

"May I ask why?"

"Well," Barrington said, "I haven't related *all* the conversation."

"Perhaps you'd better relate it all then."

"The person at the other end of the telephone

94

rather intimated that Warren felt I had been on terms of intimacy with his wife and that he was contemplating filing a divorce action."

"Under those circumstances," Mason said, "it would seem there was only one thing for you to do."

"What?"

"Contact Horace Warren and ask him frankly."

"The devil of it is," Barrington said, "I— Well, my skirts aren't entirely clean in the matter. I got mixed up in something that bothers me and I wanted to put the cards on the table with you, Mason.

"If there's anything to this preposterous story and if Horace Warren has any idea I've been involved with his wife in any way, I would— Well, it would be disastrous."

"But there *is* something you want to tell me?" Mason asked.

"Well, yes, although I came here to question *you*. You've managed to turn the tables on me."

"You wanted to tell me something," Mason reminded him.

"No, I didn't want to, I didn't intend to."

"But," Mason said, smiling, "you're going to, now. You've gone too far to stop now."

Barrington cleared his throat, shifted his position, said, "I've known Horace Warren for some time. I've been at his house two or three times, but we've never contemplated doing any business—that is, until recently."

Mason nodded.

"I got to know his wife, Lorna, and of course I got to know Judson Olney.

"About two months ago Olney came to me and asked me if I would ascertain what certain unlisted securities were worth. He thought I was in a better position to find out than he was, and I'm quite certain I was. It was a company that was operating in territory with which I was familiar and near which I had some holdings. So I made a quiet investigation and found that while the securities had no presently listed market value, there was a very high speculative value, and that a good fair average price would be around seventeen thousand dollars."

"And you so reported to Olney?"

"Yes."

"Then what happened?"

"Olney thanked me and I heard nothing more of it for a while. Then about two weeks ago Olney came to me and asked me if I could arrange to turn those securities into cash for him.

"I was instantly a little suspicious and asked him if they were his securities and if so, how he had secured them. He laughed and told me they were actually the securities of Mrs. Warren, that they represented some wildcat investment she had made, that her husband didn't like to have her making wildcat investments, but that she was always a pushover for oil developments where there was a chance to make a big killing, even if the chance was only one in a hundred thousand.

"He said that Mrs. Warren now found herself in a position where she wanted some money and didn't want her husband to know it. Therefore she wanted to sell some of her securities, ones that he didn't know she had."

"So what did you do?"

"I told Olney that I'd see what I could do. I told him I'd be willing to write my check for seventeen thousand dollars but if I had the securities transferred to my name I might do even better than that."

"So what did you do?"

"I had the securities transferred to my name and of course that started speculation on the part of other stockholders in the company who knew about the transfer. The fact that I was buying in the company made them think that they had an even better chance at success than they had realized."

"You sold the securities?" Mason asked.

"I sold them and got the wonderful price of twenty-eight thousand dollars."

"And what did you do with the money?"

"Now, there is the thing that bothers me," Barrington said. "At Olney's request I got this money in the form of cash—twenty, fifty, and one-hundred dollar bills—and turned over the cash to him."

"Did you take any steps to find out that the cash went to Mrs. Warren eventually?"

"Oh, yes. I was not that stupid, Mason. At a luncheon when I met her I asked her about it."

97

"Now, did you ask her specifically, 'Did you get the specific sum that I turned over?' or—"

"No, no, I didn't go into details. I simply told her that I felt I had secured a good price for her securities, and she told me that it was wonderful, that it was more than she had expected and that she had made a very handsome profit on the transaction, and thanked me very sweetly."

"Did she ask you not to say anything about it?"

"Actually she did. Not exactly in those words, but she told me that she couldn't ask her husband to handle the transaction because this was a speculation she had made on the side and she didn't think her husband would approve of it. She told me he didn't like her going into those highly speculative investments, or something of that sort."

"And now something has happened to make you suspicious?" Mason asked.

"Well, that phone call and Olney pulling that business about being such an old friend of your secretary and, through Miss Street, having you present at— Well, I just want to know straight out, Mason, is your connection with Warren a business connection, and if so, is there any possibility of . . . well, a divorce, and could I become involved in any way?"

Mason said, "You're a businessman, Barrington. A moment's reflection would convince you that you are coming to the wrong place to ask those questions."

"What do you mean?"

"An attorney couldn't tell you anything about his clients or about his clients' business. If you feel that Horace Warren is contemplating any legal action involving his wife, and that you might be dragged into it, the thing to do is to go to Horace Warren and ask him in so many words if he is contemplating any such action."

"And the minute I do that I let the cat out of the bag."

"Exactly," Mason said.

"I— Well, frankly, I'm worried, Mason. I can't go to Warren, you know that."

"And you know that I can't tell you what you want to know."

"Well, I was hoping you could."

"*If* I had been employed by Warren in a business relationship and Warren wanted to conceal the fact that it was a business relationship, I would hardly be in a position to blab the information to the first friend of Warren's who came to me and asked me."

"I'm not asking you to do that. I'm asking you to tell me whether . . . well, whether I'm in any sort of trouble over what I've done."

"I wouldn't think so," Mason said. "What you have done seems to me to have been open and above board, and if the circumstances are exactly as you related them to me, I can't see where anyone could take offense."

Barrington's face lit up. "Thank you very much, Mason," he said. "Thank you very much indeed. I realize that you're in a position where you can't tip your hand.''

"I can't even tell you whether my presence at that party was purely social or business," Mason said. "I can only assure you that Judson Olney came to this office to see Della Street, and told me the same story about the vacation trip, et cetera, that he subsequently told the others.''

"Then there was no business connection, no significance connected with—"

"Now, just a minute," Mason said. "I don't want you to put words in my mouth. I told you that Olney came to this office to see Miss Street. That subsequently he told me this same story.''

"All right, all right. I guess somebody has been trying to make trouble.''

"Any idea who it could be?" Mason asked.

"Well," Barrington said, "I think it was a woman. I think the attempt at disguising the voice was rather crude.''

"Any idea what woman?''

"Oh, a person always has ideas," Barrington said, making a gesture with his hand, "but those ideas don't necessarily mean anything. As you attorneys say, it takes evidence, and I wouldn't want to make any accusation, not even an intimation, without evidence.''

"In other words," Mason said, "it's now your turn to be cagey.''

Barrington got to his feet. "Thank you very much for seeing me, Mr. Mason. I am sorry that I got all worked up about this.''

"Not at all," Mason said.

"And you will regard my visit as confidential?"

Mason said, "From a social standpoint, what you have told me is confidential. From a business standpoint, I am representing clients. I have to represent those clients, and from time to time I have to give them whatever information I have uncovered."

"Now, wait a minute," Barrington said. "I didn't tell you this with the idea that you'd pass it on to any of your clients."

"Then you shouldn't have told me," Mason said. "An attorney is the representative of his clients. He is their agent. He has to play fair with them."

"Well— Oh, all right," Barrington said. "I've come to you and put my cards on the table and I'm going to leave it that way. I trust your discretion and . . . well, somehow I have an idea you won't betray my confidence unless it's necessary. Good afternoon, Mr. Mason."

"Good afternoon," Mason told him gravely.

Mason looked in the outer reception room, found that Gertie had gone home. He closed up the office and stopped by Paul Drake's office on the way to the elevator.

"Paul Drake in?" Mason asked the receptionist, who was busy at the telephone.

She nodded, gestured toward the wooden gate which led to a corridor and kept talking on the telephone.

Mason worked the concealed latch on the

wooden gate, walked down the long corridor with the rows of little cubbyhole offices on each side where operatives could interview clients or witnesses, and came to Paul Drake's office at the end of the corridor.

The office was barely large enough for Drake's desk and chair, two clients' chairs and a wastebasket. There were four telephones on Drake's desk and he was talking on one of them.

He nodded to Mason, motioned for him to sit down, and said into the telephone, "All right, see what you can find out but don't tip your hand any more than you have to. Handle it in relays and see if you can find who else is on the job. . . . I know it's difficult but do the best you can."

Drake hung up and said to Mason, "I presume you want to know if we learned anything about the man who was in your office."

"That's right," Mason said.

Drake grinned. "That guy is wearing tails like Halley's comet."

"What do you mean?" Mason asked.

"Well," Drake said, "in the first place he was wearing a rough shadow. And on a job of any real importance that means at least two smooth shadows and sometimes as many as five."

"Did your man spot the smooth shadows?"

"My *men,*" Drake said. "I put two on, with instructions to relay and telephone in information so I could be advised. . . . I can tell you this, Perry. He knows he's being shadowed, and I think he knows that my men joined in the procession, although I can't be sure because we just have to guess at those things. But he sure as hell knows there's a rough shadow on the job."

"Yes, I know he does," Mason said.

"He's staying at a little hotel here, the Exman Hotel. That's a little building they haven't got around to tearing down yet. It's sandwiched in between a couple of old-timers and the whole place is just waiting for someone to come along with a modern office building and tear the whole block down. In the meantime this Exman Hotel makes a specialty of cheap rooms."

"How's he registered?" Mason asked.

"Under the name of Newton, which I doubt very much is his real name."

"He went directly there from my office?"

"Led the whole procession of shadows directly there," Drake said. "He knows of at least one shadow but he isn't trying to ditch anybody."

Mason said, "Paul, when it comes to dealing with a blackmailer, I'm ruthless."

"Who isn't?" Drake asked.

Mason said, "I would do things that might be considered unethical if one looked at them in the cold light of business ethics."

"In dealing with a blackmailer one has to be unethical," Drake said.

Mason said, "For your information, this man's name is Collister Damon Gideon, he's a blackmailer and he's clever. Since he's just out of federal prison, he's in a vulnerable position. If it weren't for that, he'd have me crucified. I've got to run a bluff on him, but I have to play my cards as if I were holding four aces."

"Who's he blackmailing?"

"Me."

"You!" Drake said in surprise.

"That's right."

"What in the world does he have on you, Perry?"

"He doesn't have anything on me," Mason said, "but he could make an embarrassing situation by continuing to come to my office."

"Oh-oh," Drake said. "That accounts for it. The Government detectives will think some client of yours will lead them to the hidden money."

"Exactly," Mason said. "They are naturally quite interested in all the people on whom Gideon calls."

"So he has called on you, and now you're a focal point of government interest."

"Perhaps not yet," Mason said, "but if he makes repeated calls I certainly will be. It's quite possible the government will feel that I am acting as the go-between."

Drake frowned. "He's in a position to put you in one hell of a spot, Perry."

Mason nodded.

"And," Drake went on, "there's not one damned thing you can do about it. If he just wants to keep calling at your office, you can't very well stop him unless you want to make a complaint that he's attempting blackmail, and you're not in a position to do that—not if you want to protect your clients."

"That's why I said, Paul, that in dealing with a blackmailer one uses any weapon one can."

"You have some weapon in mind?" Drake asked.

Mason nodded. "You can get the original mug shots on Gideon?"

"Sure. They're in the police files."

"And you can get an artist," Mason said.

"An artist?" Drake asked.

"A police artist," Mason said. "Then get some of these police forms that they use in making composite sketches of criminals. I want a couple of real good sketches of Gideon which look pretty much like him, but I want them made in the relatively crude manner that characterizes the sketches made from the descriptions of eye-witnesses. You know how these police composite pictures are put together. Get a police artist to sketch a picture of Gideon from his mug shot so it will unmistakably be Gideon, or that is, have an unmistakable resemblance to Gideon."

"And then what?" Drake asked.

"Then," Mason said, "I'm going to give him an opportunity to get away from his shadows —both the rough shadows and the smooth shadows, so he'll be on his own."

"How are you going to do that?"

"It'll take money," Mason said. "I'm going to give him money."

"Once you start giving him money it's a one-way street," Drake said. "It's like pouring it down a rathole."

Mason shook his head and smiled. "Then when Gideon has shaken the shadows he's automatically removed any possible alibi he may have."

"And then?"

"Then," Mason said, "I'm going to flash this sketch on him and tell him that's a sketch made by a police artist from the description of an eyewitness to a holdup or murder or some crime that he will have read about in the papers."

"He'll know you're framing him," Drake said.

"He may know it but there's not a damned thing *he* can do about it," Mason said. "The weak point in the armor of a crook who has been convicted is the fact that his prior conviction can be brought out to impeach his testimony in the event he tries to deny committing the crime."

"But," Drake protested, "if he checks with police he'll find out that the sketch is purely a synthetic bit of evidence, that the police don't have that sketch in their files and—"

"A blackmailer, an ex-crook who has been to a lot of trouble to ditch the shadows, going to the police and asking them to please inspect their files?" Mason asked.

Drake thought for a minute, then broke out laughing.

"All right," he said, "you win."

"I haven't won yet," Mason said, "but I'm going to take that smooth, suave Gideon and jar him back on his heels. I told him that when it came to dealing with blackmailers I was

106

completely ruthless."

"Even so, you wouldn't frame a man for a crime he didn't commit," Drake said.

"I'm not talking about that," Mason said. "I'm talking about making him think I'm framing him for a crime that will either put him in the gas chamber or send him back to prison for life. When you start dealing with a blackmailer, Paul, there's only one thing to do and that's take the offensive."

"Okay," Drake said. "How strong do you want me to go with these shadows?"

"Keep the shadows on him," Mason said. "Get that mug shot, get the artist, and make me some police-type sketches of Gideon."

"Okay," Drake said, "will do."

Chapter Eight

WHEN MASON entered his office shortly before nine o'clock the next morning Della Street said, "How did you get along with Mr. Barrington last night? Did he cross-examine you about me?"

"No," Mason said, grinning. "I beat him to the punch and cross-examined him about him, and by the time he got done telling his story he was in such a predicament that he didn't feel like asking questions."

"Paul Drake phoned in a moment ago and said he had the sketch you wanted. What was that?"

"We'll take a look," Mason said, "and see if you recognize it. Give Paul a ring and tell him to come in."

A few moments later when Paul Drake's code knock sounded on the door, Della Street opened it.

"You've got it?" Mason asked.

"I've got it," Drake said, and handed Mason a sketch together with several photostatic copies.

Mason looked at it, smiled, and passed the

sketch over to Della Street. "Who is it, Della?"

"Why good heavens, it's that man, Gideon!"

"A darned good likeness, Paul, and the nice thing is it's handled in such a way that it looks as though it had been done by a police artist."

"It was," Drake said. "I have this friend who does this work for the police and I gave him Gideon's rap sheet. He knocked off a sketch for me from the old flier they used some time ago.

"You're dealing with a pretty hard man to bluff," Drake warned. "This fellow is above the average in intelligence, and by the time a man does time in a federal prison he soaks up enough criminal knowledge to be a match for anyone."

"Meaning me?" Mason asked.

"Well, I didn't say that," Drake said. "But don't think the guy's going to be easy, Perry."

"I don't."

The telephone rang, and Della, picking up the extension, said, "Yes, Gertie. . . . Who's calling?"

Della Street's face registered extreme annoyance. "Well, you just tell him— Wait a minute."

She placed her hand over the transmitter, said to Mason, "This man, Gideon, is on the telephone. Shall I tell Gertie to cut him off, and that we don't ever want to talk with him or—"

"Not at all," Mason said, "tell Gertie to put him on the line, and you listen in, Della."

Mason picked up the phone on his desk, said, "Hello, Mason speaking."

"Gideon," the voice at the other end of the line said. "How are you this morning, Mr. Mason?"

"Very fine, thank you."

"Well, I thought I'd drop in and see you for a little while."

"I have nothing to say to you."

"So I gathered and I presume you won't see me personally. In fact, I'm somewhat surprised that you took this telephone call. But I'll just drop in and sit in the outer office a half an hour or so and then go out again. You see, my rough shadow is still on the job and I want him to earn his money."

"By all means," Mason said.

"And," Gideon went on, "I intend to call at your office at least once a day until I find some way of shaking my shadows."

"And just how will that be?" Mason asked.

"Well," Gideon said, "as I explained to you, Mr. Mason, all effective tactics are founded on taking the initiative and doing the unexpected. If I had, say, five hundred dollars, I'd ditch all my shadows and fade out of the picture, but don't expect me to discuss my affairs on the phone. The fact that you're talking with me shows there's a recording of the conversation being made, and the fact I'm keeping on talking shows I have nothing to conceal. I want you to act for me in a certain matter and I'm coming to your office in the hope you'll see me."

Mason said, "Where are you now?"

"You know," Gideon said. "You had your

private detectives pick me up at the office and follow me last night. I came to my hotel, the Exman Hotel. I have a room here. Not much of a room but, after all, I'm not in a position at the moment to ask for the luxuries of life. I expect to be better off within the next few months. Give me an opportunity to exercise my ingenuity on the outside and I'll find something that will put me out on top, Mr. Mason. I have confidence in my own ability.''

"So I see," Mason said. "And you noticed more shadows last night?"

"Oh, Mr. Mason!" Gideon said, reproachfully, "I was loaded with them. Of course, the shadows that you had were pretty clever. They weren't like the rough shadow, but, after all, I rather expected them and that enabled me to spot them. And I even spotted a couple of the government smooth shadows. That made five people tailing me last night that I know of."

"They're waiting around outside your hotel now?" Mason asked.

"I don't find your two men," Gideon said, "and the smooth shadows are out of sight, but, of course, the rough shadow is on the job."

Mason said, "I've been thinking things over during the night."

"I was hoping you would."

"And," Mason said, "I believe you should have a chance to rehabilitate yourself. I'm sending five hundred dollars over to your hotel by messenger."

"In cash?"

"In cash.

"And," Mason told him, "I don't expect you to come near the office again. I don't want to hear from you again."

"That's right, Mr. Mason, you have my word—my word of honor."

"Thank you," Mason said. "Wait there for an hour and I'll have the money delivered."

Mason hung up the phone. "Go to the safe where we keep the emergency currency, Della. Get five hundred dollars; put it in an envelope, call a messenger and send it to Mr. Gideon at the Exman Hotel."

Drake sighed. "I hope you know what you've doing."

"What do you mean?"

"Once you give in to this guy, once he knows he can tap you for dough; once he knows that he's got something that makes you afraid of him, you'll have him on your back for the rest of your life. A blackmailer never gives up until he has bled a sucker completely white."

Mason grinned and said, "I know, but you see this five hundred dollars doesn't come out of my pocket. I am charging it to expenses and this is what I call bait. You don't catch fish by putting out a bare hook. You have to put on bait, and when you put on bait it has to be something that the fish likes. Even then you have to put it on artistically so the hook is completely covered. . . . When you come right down to it, Paul, there's

112

really quite a science to baiting a hook."

"Go on," Drake said.

"And then, after you have the hook baited, you wait until the fish takes the bait and starts off with it, and then you give a sudden jerk and your fish is hooked. If you jerk too soon, you pull the hook out of his mouth, and if you don't jerk at the right time, the fish steals the bait and leaves you with a bare hook. One has to have a sense of timing in such matters, and there is a certain amount of skill in connection with putting on the bait and hooking the fish."

"Well, you've certainly put on the bait," Drake said. "But I'll warn you, five hundred dollars will just be an entering wedge in Gideon's mind."

"He's promised me that he won't come back, or call me or get in touch with me in any way if I send over the five hundred dollars," Mason said.

Drake snorted his skeptical disbelief.

"He has," Mason said, "given me his word of honor."

Drake groaned, got to his feet, said, "Kid yourself all you want to, Perry, but don't try kidding me."

"Incidentally," Mason said, "your friend Gideon seems to be rather expert at picking up shadows. He had no difficulty whatever in picking up the two shadows you put on his tail when he left the office."

Drake made an exclamation of annoyance. "Those were pretty smooth guys," he said. "In view of the fact that a rough shadow is on the job, I didn't think Gideon would spot them."

"He spotted them," Mason said.

After a moment, Drake said, "I told you that these fellows get pretty smart while they are in stir, Perry."

"I know," Mason said, "and Gideon, I think, was rather smart to start with. Let's hope he doesn't outwit himself."

"You're really going to send that money?" Drake asked.

"I'm going to send it," Mason said. "I believe Della is putting the money in an envelope right now."

Drake said something about a fool and his money being soon parted, and left the office.

Mason looked reassuringly at Della Street as she returned with a fat envelope in her hand.

"Everything okay, Della?"

"Everything okay. The messenger is on his way up here."

"Tell him to take this envelope to Gideon at the Exman Hotel and not to bother about a receipt," Mason said.

"No receipt?" she asked. "Not even for the envelope?"

"Nothing," Mason said, grinning. "We're gentlemen, dealing with each other as such. After all, I have Mr. Gideon's word of honor."

Chapter Nine

THURSDAY MORNING Mason entered the office and asked hopefully, "What do we hear from Gideon, Della?"

"Nothing."

"No letter, no telephone?"

"Nothing."

"Perhaps an anonymous letter?"

"No, not this morning."

Mason left his desk, walked over to the window, looked down at traffic on the street below with frowning concentration.

"Should we have heard?" Della asked.

"We should have heard," Mason said. "I'm a little afraid that our friend Gideon has transferred his attentions to Mrs. Horace Warren."

The lawyer started pacing the floor, said at length, "It's inconceivable that he would have the consummate nerve to go there, yet— Ring up Paul Drake and tell him to put two *more* men on the house," Mason said. "I want the license numbers of every automobile that calls there and I want a description of every person who calls. The operatives will have to use binoculars and keep in the distance."

"Anything else?" Della asked.

"That's all," Mason said. And then added grimly, "At the moment."

By midafternoon Mason was restive, pacing the office floor, frowning, reacting nervously every time the phone rang.

At three o'clock Mason's phone rang. Della said, "Yes? Hello?" then nodded to Perry Mason.

"Gideon?" Mason asked.

"Paul Drake," she said.

Mason picked up his telephone. "Yes, Paul, what's new?"

"My face is red," Drake said.

Mason tilted back in his swivel chair, crossed his ankles on the desk, and seemed suddenly to lose all his tension.

"Why, what's the matter, Paul?" he asked solicitously.

"That damned Gideon!" Paul Drake said. "I told you that these fellows get smart in stir. This guy has become too smart for his britches."

"Meaning he was too smart for you?" Mason asked.

"He was too smart for my men," Drake said, "and then— Well, damn it, yes, Perry. He *was* too smart for me."

"What happened?" Mason asked.

"The guy went down to a used-car lot. He

116

looked over some used cars, then he purchased one and paid three hundred dollars down."

"In cash?" Mason asked.

"Of course, in cash. Hell's bells, it was out of the money you'd given him."

"Well, I'm glad to see he used it to buy something useful," Mason said. "After all, a man needs an automobile to run around in these days."

"Now, wait a minute, Perry," Paul Drake said. "This is pretty damned serious. It's a brand-new stunt as far as I'm concerned."

"Go on," Mason said. "Or why don't you come down to the office and tell me about it? Della will make you a cup of coffee and—"

"Because I don't want to face you," Drake said. "Also I'm sitting here in my office with four telephones working, trying my damnedest to get on his trail again."

"Well, what happened to the government men?" Mason asked. "Weren't they on the job?"

"My God," Drake said, "there were three government smooth shadows on the job, one rough shadow and my two shadows. That made six shadows that were tailing that bird."

"And he walked away from all of them?"

"I'll say he did."

"What did he do?"

"Well, he got this automobile, made a down payment on it, signed the contract, and started out.

"Of course we felt that since he had that

117

automobile it was going to be the old run-around, that he'd go through signals just as they were changing and all that stuff. My men felt that way about it and apparently the government men did, too."

"How do you handle a situation of that sort?" Mason asked.

"With enough shadows, it's a cinch," Drake said. "We had one shadow get ahead of him and one stay behind him. We had him bracketed. Then whenever we'd come to an intersection with a signal one of my men would go ahead and the other would stay behind. And of course the rough shadow stayed behind. In that way if Gideon went through a signal just as it was changing, or took a chance on running a red light, the shadows could wait patiently behind because there were shadows ahead to pick him up."

"What about the government men?"

"They were playing it the same way," Drake said. "My men spotted at least one of the government men, and that government man had spotted him, because he gave him the high sign."

"And Gideon got away from a deal of that sort?" Mason asked.

"I'll say he got away from it."

"How?"

"He ditched the rough shadow and one of the smooth shadows," Drake said. "He seemed to feel he had it made. He drove to the airport, parked the car with the motor running and tipped an attendant to let it stay there for five minutes."

"Go on," Mason said.

"Well, that was a cinch," Drake said. "The remaining government men came up and made a kick about the car being there in a place where there was supposed to be no parking. They squawked a little bit and insisted the attendant drive it away.

"While they were doing all this, of course, they were putting an electric bug on the car so they could follow him without crowding him. With one of those electric bugs you can be several blocks away and still follow a guy."

"Go on," Mason said, "what happened? Did they follow him in to the air terminal?"

"No, they didn't," Drake said, "because when a man has just paid three hundred dollars down on an automobile you don't think he's going to walk away and leave it with the motor running."

Mason started to laugh.

"Go ahead and laugh, damn it!" Drake said irritably.

"So you don't know where he went?" Mason asked.

"Of course we know where he went," Drake said. "We're not that dumb. We didn't follow him into the air terminal but we went in and started milling around and we watched every outgoing plane that was scheduled to depart within the next thirty minutes."

"Well," Mason said, "if he went in, he had to come out."

"He went out all right," Drake said. "He

119

walked right out the door, met another guy, identified himself, and they walked twenty yards to a helicopter that was sitting there with the motor running. They both got in and the helicopter took off and we were left on the ground gawking.''

''Couldn't follow him?'' Mason asked.

''How the hell you going to follow a helicopter out of a busy airport,'' Drake asked, ''unless you have another helicopter on the job?

''We did everything we could. We got the tower and told them to order the helicopter to come back. We got another helicopter warmed up, but of course Gideon expected all that. He had the helicopter go for about three minutes, then told the pilot to land him in a vacant field by a boulevard where there was a good line of buses.

''The pilot did that and was just getting in the air coming back when he heard the tower calling him to return at once. Of course the tower felt that the helicopter pilot might have the radio on the loud-speaker so that his passenger could hear everything that was being said, so the tower was very mysterious. They told him that because of an emergency, and apparently because part of his gear was not in order, he was to return at once and make a cautious landing.

''So the guy returned and— Well, that's all there is to it. The shadows are sitting on an empty car. Gideon's gone.''

''What about the car?'' Mason asked. ''Don't they sign a contract that they have to keep up payments and if they make false representations don't they—"

"Oh, shucks," Drake said, "Gideon's too damned smart for that. Within twenty minutes after he'd given us the slip at the airport he called the used-car dealer, told him where he'd left the car, told him to go get it and repossess it. He said that after thinking things over he'd realized that he had no business buying the car in the first place, that he wasn't going to have enough use for it, that something else had come up and a friend had a car he could borrow. He told the startled used-car dealer that they'd just call the whole transaction off, that he wouldn't try to collect back any of his down payment because he realized it was his mistake, and all that stuff."

"And the car dealer fell for it?"

"Sure, he fell for it. Told him that was very generous of him, said that if he sold the car within the next couple of days he'd be able to make some kind of refund on Gideon's down payment, thanked him a lot and went out and got the car."

Mason's laugh died down to a chuckle.

"I'm glad it amuses you," Drake said stiffly.

"I remember," Mason said, "you told me not to let Gideon outsmart me, that those fellows got pretty slick after they'd been in prison and that I'd have to watch my step. Apparently you should have been taking some of your own advice."

"Oh, go to hell," Drake said irritably.

"Well," Mason said, "he's played right into

our hands now."

"What do you mean?" Drake asked.

Mason said, "As long as he had shadows on his tail he had a perfect alibi."

"Alibi for what?" Drake asked.

"For anything," Mason said. "He couldn't be accused of committing a crime because he'd simply call the shadows to the stand, ask them where he was when the crime was committed and that would be that. I told you, once he'd lost his shadows he'd have no alibi."

There was silence on the telephone while Drake was thinking that over.

"So the five hundred dollars *was* good bait."

Mason said, "I'm making no comments, Paul, but from now on start keeping track of every unsolved crime committed in the city, that is, every major crime, particularly the murders and the murder stick-ups where there are witnesses.

"Whenever you find one of those crimes, have one of your men take that police sketch, go to the eyewitnesses and ask them if that doesn't look like the man they saw at the scene of the crime."

"And try to convince them that it's the man they saw?"

"Oh, nothing like that," Mason said. "Nothing crude, but just plant the idea in their minds that someone, at least, thinks this man is suspect. Then if anything should happen we could of course claim that we were acting in good faith, trying to solve crimes of violence.

"You see, as far as I'm concerned, Paul, here is

a man with a criminal record who is at least short of money. He might well turn to crime."

"Short of money, my eye," Drake said. "The guy's smoking fifty-cent cigars and wearing a two-hundred-and-fifty-dollar suit of clothes. That's what made the government men so mad. The guy walked right into the best clothing store, big as life, and got the best suit they had in the place."

"And the government men have no idea where he got the money?"

"Not the slightest. He must have picked it out of thin air because they've been shadowing him from the time he left prison."

Mason thought that over for a moment, then again chuckled. "Things are looking better every minute, Paul. Keep in touch with me."

Chapter Ten

LATE FRIDAY morning Mason's phone rang and Paul Drake said, "Perry, I'm getting frightened."

"How come?" Mason asked.

"That confounded identification business. I'm afraid we're in a jam."

"Now look," Mason told him, "all we have to do is to act in good faith so that we're not lying to Gideon. We simply tell him that this picture of him has been submitted to the eyewitnesses in a murder case. He, of course, has no idea that *we* ordered the picture made. He thinks it's a composite picture made from the description of eyewitnesses—not a picture that we had made and then submitted to eyewitnesses.

"The guy is smart. Knowing what would happen to him when he gets on the witness stand and his past record comes out, he's going to take it on the lam. We won't hear any more from him."

"You don't know the half of it," Drake said.

"All right, what's the half of it?"

124

"You know Farley Fulton, my operative?"

"I've met him, yes. Seems like a pretty level-headed sort of a chap."

"All right," Drake said. "The Pacific Northern Supermarket was robbed last night. They got away with about seven thousand dollars. There was a night watchman on duty, and evidently he surprised the burglar."

"More than one?" Mason asked.

"Apparently a lone wolf."

"All right, what happened?"

"He gunned the watchman and then escaped through the front door."

"How bad is it?" Mason asked. "The watchman, I mean."

"The watchman is going to live. Fellow by the name of Steven Hooks. The bullet was aimed right for the heart, but it was deflected from his shield. Gave him a nasty shoulder wound and knocked him off his feet, but he's okay."

"All right," Mason said, "what are you getting at?"

"Well, I followed your instructions. Had Fulton take this sketch of Gideon to the watchman and the other eyewitness, a fellow by the name of Drew Kearny.

"Now, Kearny was a fellow who had been at a late motion picture show and happened to be walking down the street just as this holdup man burst out the front door. He threw a gun on Kearny, told him to stick up his hands. Kearny thought it was a holdup but the fellow just used the gun to terrorize Kearny, then sprinted across the street and into an alley.

"Kearny started trying to find a phone where he could call police, but as it happened someone had already heard the gunshot and telephoned the police. A police cruiser came along so Kearny flagged them down and gave them his story and a description of the guy. It was a pretty good description. He claims he got a good look at him."

"Look anything like Gideon?" Mason asked.

"Two eyes, a nose and a mouth, and that's all the resemblance."

"But that doesn't keep us from showing him the sketch," Mason said, "and we can plant a story in the paper that the police artist has made a composite sketch—"

"Wait a minute, you haven't heard anything," Drake said. "We showed Kearny the sketch and he just laughed at us, said it had no resemblance whatever to the fellow, that the stick-up was an older man, more heavy-set, that the eyes were different, and so forth. So then Farley Fulton got into the hospital and showed the sketch to Steven Hooks.

"Now, Fulton claims that he didn't use any suggestion, that he just told Hooks he'd like to have him look over this sketch and see if there was any resemblance and all that."

"All right," Mason said, "what are you getting at?"

"Hooks says it looks like the guy."

"What!" Mason exclaimed.

"Well, he can't exactly identify him, but he said the sketch looked very much like the man, although he had only the one fleeting glimpse of him before the shooting started. There was a night light on. Hooks first saw the fellow's back. He made the mistake of yelling before he had his gun out. He was drawing his gun and yelling at the same time. The holdup man had his gun out. He whirled and fired and the shot hit Hooks a glancing blow on the shield and down he went. He wasn't in a position to get a very good look at the man.

"On the other hand, this fellow Kearny, who was walking along the street when the fellow burst out of the door, was within eight or ten feet of the guy and had a good chance to see his face.

"So now we're in the devil of a fix. The police have learned from Hooks that a private detective agency had a sketch that looked something like the holdup man and they want the sketch and want to know what it's all about. I'm keeping Fulton under cover. I told the police he's out on a job. They want to see him as soon as he comes in. I'm afraid there's hell to pay."

"That," Mason said, "is an unexpected complication. What about this fellow, Drew Kearny?"

"That's why I've called you," Drake said. "He's in the office. He wants to take another look at the sketch. He says he doesn't think it's the same guy, but the watchman told him he

127

thought the sketch looked like the guy, so Kearny wants to take another look."

"He's in your office now?"

"Yes."

"Where's the sketch?"

"I have a photostatic copy."

"Bring it down," Mason said, "and bring Kearny along with it. Let *me* talk with him."

"I was hoping you'd do that," Drake said. "I was hoping you'd take over on this, but we've got to turn that sketch over to the police sooner or later, Perry."

Mason said, "We'll cross that bridge when we come to it. My own inclination is to turn it over to them. Let's talk with Kearny and see if we can't make something out of that."

"Be right down," Drake said.

Mason hung up the telephone and turned to Della, who had been monitoring the conversation.

"Now we're in a jam," he said. "That damned watchman. . . . Of course, that's one of the things that happens with eyewitness identification. That's why it's the most unreliable type of evidence we have. Suggestion, self-hypnosis, tricky recollection, poor observation; everything enters into it and a good percentage of the time someone, acting in the highest good faith, comes along with a cockeyed identification."

Drake's code knock sounded on the door. Mason let him in.

Drake turned to the man with him and said, "This is Drew Kearny, Mr. Mason."

128

"How are you, Mr. Kearny?" Mason said, shaking hands.

Kearny, a man in his early forties, with steady gray eyes, a strong, determined mouth, broad shoulders, and something of a paunch, said, "How do you do, sir? I've heard a great deal about you and it's a real pleasure to meet you."

"Sit down, sit down," Mason said. "Make yourselves comfortable. Now, what is all this about, Paul?"

Drake said, "Drew Kearny had been at a late movie and was coming past the Pacific Northern Supermarket on his way home a little after midnight. The door burst open and a man ran out. Kearny found himself looking into the business end of a gun. He automatically stuck his hands up, and because he was carrying a fairly large sum of money, figured he was going to be held up. But the fellow simply kept the gun pointed at him and said, 'Keep your hands up,' then backed away until he was halfway across the street, turned and ran through an alley.

"Kearny felt, of course, something was wrong and tried the door of the supermarket but it had a spring lock on it and it had swung shut and latched. So Kearny started running down the street, looking for the nearest telephone he could use. He's— Well, you tell it, Kearny."

Kearny patted his stomach. "I'm not as much of a sprinter as I used to be. I slowed down after about a couple of blocks and was walking along, trying to remember where the nearest phone was."

"You're familiar with the neighborhood?" Mason asked.

"Fairly familiar. My place of business is not too far away."

"What's your business?"

"Electrical repairing."

"All right," Mason said, "what happened?"

"Well, as luck would have it, I saw a flashing red light and a police car came along fast. I ran out in the middle of the street and flagged them down. I told them what had happened and they put out a general alarm and threw a cordon around the district, but I guess they didn't get the guy. And of course they went on into the supermarket and found the watchman, who was pretty badly knocked out but in a short time they had him out and hospitalized.

"Now, what's bothering me is this sketch that this detective showed me. Of course it's awfully hard to remember people when you get just a quick glance of them, particularly during a time of excitement, but I'm pretty good that way. I seldom forget a face, and I had a *good* look at this guy."

"And you saw the sketch?" Mason asked.

"I saw the sketch."

"Any chance it's the same man?"

Kearny said, "I didn't think so, but I don't want to give any crook the breaks. I talked with the watchman, and I decided I'd better study that sketch."

"Oh, well," Mason said, "these things happen every once in a while. Something goes wrong with an identification and—"

"That's not the point," Kearny said. "I'm a law-abiding citizen and I hate crooks and I hate stick-ups. I've been held up once, lost more money than I could afford to lose.

"Now, when this detective first identified himself and asked me to take a look at that sketch, I took a quick look at him and told him hell no, that wasn't the man at all, and I didn't think much more of it, but I did take the precaution of getting the guy's card so I could get in touch with him later if anything happened."

"The police had been asking you for a detailed description?" Mason asked.

"Sure they had. I was with the police for more than two hours and they had an artist working on the description I gave them."

"Well then, that's all there is to it," Mason said.

"No, it isn't," Kearny said, "because I understand now the watchman said that sketch looked a lot like the fellow, so I want to take another look at it and check. I'd sure hate to let a crook get away."

Mason said, "You have that sketch, Paul?"

Drake hesitated perceptibly, then said, "Yes, I have a copy."

"Let's take a look," Mason said.

Mason spread a copy of the sketch of Collister

Gideon out on the desk. "Take a look," he said.

Kearny studied it carefully, then said, "Well, it's hard to say. What the watchman says has given me a jolt. I got sort of uncertain, but now I know this isn't the guy. The fellow I saw was older, he was heavier, he was . . . well, sort of menacing. This fellow looks more the intellectual type. This guy that came busting out of there was a thug."

"Of course," Mason said, "experience shows that in times of emotional disturbance of that sort, particularly where a man has a gun, the witnesses are inclined to think the man is bigger than he actually is, heavier than he actually is, and quite frequently, older than he actually is."

"Well, I couldn't make *that* much of a mistake," Kearny said. "It's all right. I just wanted to satisfy myself and I don't know what all the blinking fuss is about. Hell's bells, I just came up to this detective's office to check to see if I'd made a mistake, after I heard the watchman said the sketch was one that looked to him like the fellow."

"No chance *you* could be mistaken?" Mason asked.

"I saw the fellow real close. Had a good look at him. This sketch— No, this isn't the guy."

"Is there perhaps some slight resemblance here which confused the watchman?" Mason asked.

Kearny said, "Of course there is. Otherwise he wouldn't have thought it was the guy." He looked at the sketch again and covered up the lower part.

"The mouth is the thing that doesn't click," he said. "The eyes aren't so bad, but this fellow had a mouth that was—I don't know what was wrong with it. Maybe he was holding something in his mouth, but the upper part of this sketch could be— Well, it's something like the guy. . . . That's what keeps bothering me. I have a feeling I've seen this bird somewhere before but . . ." He broke off and shook his head. "Anyhow, I can't identify this sketch as being that of the man."

"All right," Mason told him. "That's as far as we can go. Thanks a lot for coming in."

"Who is this fellow? Where did you get the picture?" Kearny asked.

Mason said, "We're interested in certain aspects of crime. That is, of course, the Drake Detective Agency is. And in the course of its investigations it— Well, of course, they run into lots of peculiar things."

Mason smiled and extended his hand. "Nice to have met you, Mr. Kearny."

Kearny grinned and said, "Okay, don't tell me if you don't want to. That's the best piece of double-talk I've heard in a long while. Thanks a lot, Mr. Drake. You have my address. Good-by, everyone."

Kearny went out.

Drake mopped his forehead. "What a hell of a mess we're in. The watchman told the police we had a sketch of the burglar."

"Can't you get to that watchman and throw cold water on his identification?"

133

"It wasn't an identification," Drake said. "He said there was a strong resemblance and let it go at that."

"Well, can't you get him to back up a little bit in view of what Kearny says?"

"I probably could," Drake said, "but it's too hot right now. The police are wondering what in hell we're trying to do."

"Well, let the police worry about their end of the business," Mason said, "and we'll worry about ours."

"Suppose they call on me and want to see the sketch?"

"Show it to them."

"Then they'll ask where I got it."

"Tell them an artist drew it."

"They'll want to know the artist."

"Refer them to me."

"That damned watchman," Drake said moodily. "He's really got us in a spot."

Mason said, "Don't overlook the fact that this plays right into our hands. It gives us a beautiful club. We'll let the police take this sketch, and if the watchman does keep insisting it looks like the man, the police will publish it, Gideon will take one agonized look at the newspaper and be on his way out of the country just as fast as he can go."

"What'll he use for funds?" Drake asked.

"Whatever he can scrape up," Mason said thoughtfully. "And that raises a point I'd better think about."

Chapter Eleven

IT HAD started to cloud up that morning and by noon a cold, sullen rain was falling. At one o'clock Drake called to report Mrs. Warren had gone out in her car, and his men had lost her.

"Was she trying to shake loose from them?" Mason asked.

"I don't think so, Perry. My men don't think she even knew she was wearing a tail. She just made a sudden left turn from a right-hand lane, and my men were boxed in where they couldn't get over in time to follow. They tried the next intersection, but they didn't pick her up again.

"Those things sometimes happen to even the best shadows in the business. She'll be back and the men at the house will pick her up again."

"I know," Mason said, "but what mischief will she get into in the meantime?"

"Oh, she's just gone shopping," Drake said.

"Let's hope so," Mason told him. "Keep me posted, Paul."

The lawyer hung up.

At two o'clock Mason's phone rang again.

Della Street answered the phone, frowned, put her hand over the transmitter and said to Perry Mason, "This is Gideon."

Mason's face broke into a grin. "The shoe is beginning to pinch," he said. "Put him on."

Mason picked up the telephone. "Yes, what is it, Gideon?"

Gideon's voice was as smooth as the purring of a contented cat. "Mr. Mason," he said, "I hadn't intended to bother you again, but a matter has come up which leaves me no alternative."

"Go ahead," Mason said.

"I am taking the precaution of using a telephone booth," Gideon said, "although I hardly think that is necessary. I'm quite certain that I have ditched not only the rough shadows and the smooth shadows of the government, but the two men that your detective agency had on me."

"Go ahead," Mason said. "What do you want?"

"To be perfectly crude, and come to the point rather quickly, which I am forced to do because I don't want you to try to trace this call, I want ten thousand dollars."

"I thought perhaps it would come to this," Mason said.

"I'm sorry," Gideon said, "but I have an opportunity to leave the country and engage in business on foreign soil. I need some operating capital to get there. Now, of course, Mr. Mason, I

136

don't expect you to furnish this capital, but you have a client who I am quite certain would be only too glad to have me completely out of the United States.''

"All right," Mason said, "where are you?"

"Not where I am," Gideon said, "but where I am going to be. What time do you have?"

"A little after two o'clock," Mason said. "I—"

"Never mind that 'little after' business. I want the exact time. What time do you have?"

"Six minutes past two."

"Congratulations on your watch. You are within thirty seconds of complete accuracy.

"Here is what you do," Gideon said. "You get ten thousand dollars in bills, none of which are more than fifty dollars in denomination. Mostly I want twenties."

"You can save your breath," Mason said. "I don't do business with blackmailers and I'm not going to any bank."

Gideon kept on as though there had been no interruption. "Put these bills in a bag, preferably a rather small bag—one that will just hold them. You had better take a pencil to jot down this address because I'm going to make this phone call very short and I'm not going to repeat. At the corner of Clovina and Hendersell there's a vacant store building with a warehouse in back. It has signs *For Lease* in the front. The front door is closed. The alley turns off of Hendersell and the back door leading to the alley is open. The building has been vacant for some time. It's

137

involved in litigation. It's rather a disreputable neighborhood and you'll probably hesitate about turning in to the alley. You had better come armed, since you are carrying a large sum of money, and you may be traced from the bank."

"I'm not going to come and I'm not going to carry any large sum of money," Mason said.

"If," Gideon went on, heedless of the interruption, "you would like to have someone with you as a bodyguard, that's all right provided he does not get out of the car. You and you alone are to enter the back door of that storeroom at precisely twenty minutes past three. That will give you time to look up the location on the map, go to the bank, and get the money. You'll probably need an authorization from your client in order to get it, although I think you have blanket instructions to do anything that's necessary."

Mason said, "Look, Gideon, as I told you, there are three ways of dealing with a blackmailer. One, you pay off. Two, you go to the police. Three, you see that the blackmailer is no longer around."

"I'm not going to be around. I told you that."

"That wasn't what I meant," Mason said. "I meant exactly what I said. You see the blackmailer is no longer around."

"Thinking of killing me?" Gideon asked in a bantering tone of voice.

"Exactly," Mason said.

"What form of weapon would you use?"

"The law."

"The law? Are you kidding?"

"I'm *deadly* serious," Mason said. "A supermarket was entered last night. A watchman surprised the thief and was shot. He may die. The burglar, still brandishing a gun, ran from the store and was seen by a reputable witness. I happen to have in my possession a composite sketch which was made by a police artist, and you'd be surprised at the resemblance to your face. I don't think there's any question but that the witnesses will identify you."

"Why you . . . you—!"

"Once you are arrested for murder," Mason went on, "you have to take the stand to proclaim your innocence. Then the district attorney asks you if, as a matter of fact, you haven't been convicted of a felony and you have to admit that you have been so convicted. The jury takes one good long look at you and that's all that is needed."

"Now, you look here," Gideon said, "you can't do this. I'll tell everything I know. I'll get on the stand, relate this telephone conversation and—"

"And it will be so fantastic," Mason interrupted, "that no one will believe you. But the effect of it will be that you'll have to claim that I tried to frame a murder on you because you were blackmailing a client of mine. Think *that* over."

"I— You—"

"And on second thought," Mason said, "since you have given me a place to meet you, I'll be

139

there at exactly twenty minutes past three. I won't be bringing any money and I *will* have a gun."

Mason hung up the telephone.

Della Street, who had been monitoring the conversation, looked at Perry Mason with wide eyes. "Do you, by any chance, want to go to the bank and get some money, just in case—"

"No, thanks," Mason said.

"Are you going alone?" she asked apprehensively.

Mason said, "A blackmailer doesn't want a witness and when I'm dealing with a blackmailer I don't want one. I'm rather good at making threats myself. . . . Where's the reproduction of that composite sketch Paul Drake had the police artist make? Here's where I jar a blackmailer right back on his heels and start him running so far and so fast he won't ever come back."

Mason pushed back his chair, stood at the desk, his clenched fists pressing down on the blotter, his chin jutting forward with grim determination.

"Della," he said, "ring Horace Warren's office, tell his secretary you're a reporter with one of the wire services, that you'd like a brief interview in connection with some matter that originated in the east and your editor has instructed you to get an immediate interview."

Della Street put through the call, listened, said, "Thank you," hung up, turned to Mason and said, "Out on an important appointment. Won't be back until after four this afternoon."

Mason said, "Now call for your friend, Judson

Olney. Tell whoever answers that you're his friend, Della Street, and that he left word for you to call."

Again Della put through the call. Again she said, "Thank you," and turned to Mason. "He's out until three-thirty. I think that was the secretary. Her tone was acid."

Mason stood in frowning contemplation.

"Damn Paul Drake's men for losing Mrs. Warren," he said at length, "but it doesn't make any difference. We know now where she's going—and there isn't time to head her off."

Della Street's face showed dismay. "Do you think she's heading for a rendezvous with Gideon?"

"Where else?" Mason asked. "If Gideon tried putting the bite on me, it's almost certain he's trying Mrs. Warren. He's worked out a schedule. Probably Mrs. Warren at two-thirty, Horace Warren at two-forty-five, Olney at three, me at three-twenty—a plane at four-thirty. And I can't stop him. There isn't time. That place is at the other end of town."

"Couldn't Paul Drake get some men there and—"

"There isn't time," Mason said. "We're dealing with a super-intelligent crook and so far he's had all the breaks."

"Don't you think you jolted him with what you said about the witnesses in that murder case?"

"Of course I jolted him," Mason said, "but I could tell from his manner that it doesn't make as much difference as I'd hoped. He's cleaning up. He's putting the bite on everybody. He's going to get the most he can and then clear out.''

"And you can't stop him?"

"I can't stop him," Mason said, "because I don't dare to let him be picked up by the police and he knows it. Nevertheless, I don't want to sit idly by and have him put his blackmail scheme into operation."

"Will you wait until three-twenty to—"

"No," Mason interrupted. "That's where I have him. His split-second timing shows that he's working out a very carefully engineered schedule for getting his victims on the spot one at a time and—Della, ring up the fire department. Put in a fire alarm for the store at the corner of Clovina and Hendersell. Tell them there's a big fire in the back room."

Della Street's eyes were wide. "That's a crime. That—"

"Sure, it's a crime," Mason said. "It's also a crime to exceed the speed limit and that's what I'm going to do getting there. I defy any blackmailer to carry on a successful blackmail approach in the midst of a fire alarm.

"Then get Paul Drake to send two operatives down to Clovina and Hendersell just as fast as he can!"

"I'm on my way."

Mason grabbed his hat and shot out of the door.

Chapter Twelve

MASON PARKED his car on Clovina Avenue.

On the other side of the street were two police cars and the red car of a deputy fire chief. Further down the block there were several cars parked at the curb.

The store at the corner of Clovina and Hendersell had evidently been a large space, low rental property. The building was run-down, the neighborhood was drab and dejected. At one time the building had been used for surplus goods, and a weather-beaten sign of SURPLUS SALE still adorned the front of the building.

As Mason left the car a man came up to him. "Perry Mason?"

"That's right."

"I'm Lou Pitman, one of Drake's operatives. Drake caught me on the car radio phone and sent me here on a rush call. As it happened I was working on another job not too far away and I got here about the same time the fire department did."

Mason eyed the man steadily. "Let's see your credentials," he said.

Pitman produced his identification card.

"Okay," Mason said. "Now tell me what happened."

"It was a false alarm," Pitman said. "The fire company came charging up, parked their fire trucks, looked the place over, started to leave, then one of them looked in a window, said something to the others. They knocked a window out, went in, then evidently put in a call over their short-wave radio for the police. The police came rushing out here and apparently there was a man trapped inside the building."

"Trapped inside the building?" Mason asked.

"That's right."

"He didn't get away?"

"He didn't get away."

"He should have," Mason said thoughtfully. "He shouldn't have been there by the time the fire wagons got there. Go on, what happened?"

"I don't know what happened, but more police cars have been coming. There's something on the inside there that bothers them and they're evidently questioning this man— Here they come now."

The front door of the store opened. Lt. Tragg, flanked by a plain-clothes detective and two uniformed officers, escorted Horace Warren out of the building.

"Good Lord!" Mason said.

"You know him?" Pitman asked.

Abruptly Mason turned from Pitman, barged across the street and moved toward the group.

One of the officers said something to Lt. Tragg, who looked up and was unable to keep the expression of surprise from his face as he saw Mason bearing down on them.

"Well, well," Tragg said. "This is quick work! How did you get here? Did your client telephone you and—"

Mason fastened his eyes on Warren. "Not one word, Warren," he said. "Not one word. *Don't open your lips!*"

One of the uniformed officers barged forward, shoved Mason back. "On your way," he said, "this is a homicide."

"Not one word," Mason called over his shoulder. Then said to the officer, "I'm this man's attorney."

"I don't give a damn who you are," the officer told him. "After he's booked he has the right to ask for a lawyer and you can come and see him, but you're not going to butt in on things here. On your way!"

Mason side-stepped enough to catch Warren's eye and received a slight nod of the head.

Mason walked back across the street.

The other group entered two police cars and roared away.

"Wasn't that Tragg, of Homicide?" Pitman asked.

"That's right," Mason said. "He wouldn't be here unless there was a dead body inside and unless it was murder.

"They're leaving a police car there with officers in charge of the place. That looks like a big storeroom with a warehouse in back. There may be an entrance on the other street. As soon as you get reinforcements here, cover the building. Try and find out what happened and telephone me at my office."

Mason walked dejectedly across to his car, got in, twisted the ignition key, started the motor and drove back toward his office.

Chapter Thirteen

DELLA STREET looked up in surprise as Mason entered the office.

"What's the matter, didn't you get down there?" she asked.

"I got down there," Mason said, "and I got back. Now I'm waiting for a telephone call."

Della raised inquiring eyebrows.

"I think," Mason said, "we'll have a call from Horace Warren within a short time. He'll want me to represent him on a charge of murder."

"Murder!" Della echoed.

"That's right," Mason said. "Apparently he got down to Gideon before I did. He had the same idea I did, that in dealing with a blackmailer there were only three possible channels of approach—and one of them is to kill him."

"And you mean Warren decided to kill him?"

"Apparently Warren thought he could get away with it," Mason said, "and he might have if it hadn't been for that damned fire alarm we turned in."

"Oh-oh," Della Street said.

"He and Gideon were probably alone," Mason said. "They had a showdown. Warren killed him, and I can't blame him very much for that. But then he heard the sirens of the fire department and was trapped in the building. They caught him red-handed."

"What about Mrs. Warren?"

"She had either been there before we sewed the building up with the fire alarm, or else she didn't get there until afterwards. And of course at that time the building was under police guard.

"She's smart enough to have spotted the uniformed police there and gone on home. Now, Della, that's where you come in. Get in your car, go out to the house. See if Mrs. Warren is home. If she is, deliver your message. If she isn't, wait until she gets home and tell her not to say a word to anyone about anything. Simply state that she is making no comment *about anything* until she has had a chance to talk with an attorney."

"With you?" Della asked.

"You don't have to say with me," Mason said. "I'd prefer you didn't. She can simply tell the police that she wants to talk with an attorney. I *think* I'm going to be representing her husband."

"But if they caught him red-handed," Della Street ventured, "what can you—"

"I don't know," Mason said. "But Gideon was certainly asking for it."

The telephone rang.

Della picked up the telephone, said, "Yes,

Gertie. . . . Yes, Mr. Mason will talk."

She turned. "Horace Warren now," she said.

Mason picked up the telephone. "Yes, Warren."

"I'm being held on a charge of murder. They say I have a right to telephone an attorney and—"

"I'll be there within fifteen minutes," Mason said. "Don't tell them anything. You understand? Not one single damned thing."

"I understand."

"I'll be there," Mason said.

Chapter Fourteen

MASON SAT in the counsel room and said to Horace Warren, "Keep your voice down. Put your mouth close to my ear and mumble the words. I've always had a feeling this room was bugged. Now first, answer some of my questions. Did you take the money out of the suitcase in your wife's bedroom?"

"Yes."

"Why?"

"Because I knew it was blackmail and I didn't want her to pay blackmail. I felt that if I stole the money and left nothing but newspapers in the suitcase, when she tried to pay the blackmailer she would find she had been robbed and would then come to me and confide in me."

"Did she?"

"No."

"What did she do?"

"Apparently she went about getting another batch of money together."

"Did you know who was putting the bite on her?"

"Yes."

"How long had you known?"

"I knew before I married her, Mr. Mason. But she didn't know I knew it and if she wanted it a secret I decided to help her keep that secret."

"How did you know about it?"

"Through Judson Olney."

"What did he know?"

"He knew who she was."

"How did he know?"

"When I met Lorna in Mexico City and became interested in her, I could tell that there was something in her past that was bothering her. She just never talked about her past, and I could see she was in a panic.

"At that time, Judson Olney was my legman. He was my secretary and did all my legwork. I told him to find out about Lorna Neely, put him on a plane and told him to get the information.

"It wasn't hard to get. On the other hand, she hadn't been implicated in anything. She had been the innocent tool of a smooth crook who had wormed his way into her confidence and had profited by her loyalty."

"Do you think she took that forty-seven thousand to keep for him?"

"I never thought so until . . . . well, until I knew that he was getting out of prison and—Well, she had forty-seven thousand dollars in the suitcase."

"So now you think she acted as custodian of

that money for him?"

"I don't know."

"Does it make any difference in the way you feel toward her?"

"No."

"All right. Now tell me what happened," Mason said, "and remember to keep your voice low, put your mouth close to my ear and mumble."

"Gideon was making a cleanup," Warren said. "I suppose he telephoned Lorna. He telephoned Judson Olney. He telephoned me. He put the bite on everyone. He said he was leaving and he needed cash money."

"Why Olney?" Mason asked.

"Olney is very loyal to my interests. He didn't know all that was going on but he was terribly afraid that Gideon was going to blackmail Lorna and the story might come out. Gideon put a very gentle touch on him, just twenty-five hundred dollars."

"How much on you?"

"He wanted me to get ten thousand in cash and bring it to him."

"He told you who he was?"

"Yes."

"Did he tell you of his connection with your wife?"

"He told me the whole thing over the telephone. The man was fiendish, Mason."

"Then it's logical to assume he telephoned your wife."

"I presume so."

"And she went out there with money?"

"I don't know."

"Did Olney go out there with money?"

"Olney was raising the money."

"Did Olney say anything to you?"

"Not at first. He was trying to raise the money. The cashier told me that Olney wanted an advance. I called him in and asked him what was the matter and finally I became convinced it was blackmail, and knowing what Gideon had been up to I faced Olney. He then admitted that it was true, that he was trying to protect Lorna and protect me. The man has that much loyalty."

"You trust him?" Mason asked. "You think it's simply loyalty?"

"I think it's simply loyalty."

"What did you tell him?"

"I told him to forget it, that I'd take care of it, and I went down there."

"Did you have the money?" Mason asked.

"No, I didn't have the money. I knew that if I once started paying him there'd be no end to it."

"In dealing with a blackmailer," Mason said, "you either submit to his demands, you call in the police, or you kill him. Now then, you weren't going to pay his demands. Did you make up your mind you were going to kill him?"

"No, Mr. Mason, I didn't. I decided to take the second choice. I decided to tell him that if he made any other demand I was going to go to the police, tell them the whole story, accuse him of blackmailing and put him back in prison."

"And what did he say when you put that up to him?" Mason asked.

"He never had a chance. He was dead when I got there."

Mason raised his eyebrows.

"I know it sounds strange," Warren said, "but he was dead. Someone had killed him."

"Do you know how?"

"I assume with a revolver. There was a revolver there on the table."

"The police found it?" Mason asked.

Warren lowered his eyes.

"Well?" Mason asked.

"I lost my head, Mason."

"What the devil!" Mason said. "Come clean. What happened?"

"The man was lying there dead. He had evidently been living there for some time. It was a secret hide-out. There were cases of canned goods and a little alcohol stove, a table, a box filled with empty tin cans, and, as I say, there was this gun on the table."

"Don't tell me you touched that gun," Mason said.

"I did worse than that," Warren said. "When I arrived at the warehouse I found a door open. I walked in. At first I didn't see anyone. I saw this gun on the table and I picked it up. I hadn't armed myself before going there, but I felt that it would be a good plan to disarm my adversary. So I put the gun in my pocket."

"Then what?"

"Then I walked around behind a box of canned goods and saw Gideon lying there on the floor and at that moment sirens seemed to explode all over the place. Naturally I thought it was the police. Actually it was the fire department. I lost my head, turned and ran, and tried to conceal myself in the warehouse. They found me."

Mason said, "Damn it, Warren, quit lying to me! You're not that simple."

"I'm telling you the facts."

"No, you're not," Mason said. "You're telling me the story. You thought Lorna had killed him, didn't you?"

"I . . . I've told you what happened."

"No, you haven't. There was something there that made you think Lorna had killed him. What was it?"

Warren hesitated, then said, "I saw Lorna's car as I turned down Clovina Avenue."

"Did she see you?"

"No."

"How far was that from the scene of the crime?"

"Five or six blocks."

"Anything else?" Mason asked.

"One of Lorna's gloves was on the floor, right by the table."

"Which one, left or right?"

"I don't know."

"How do you know it was Lorna's?"

"It was a very unusual shade for suède."

"And what did you do with it?" Mason asked.

"I picked it up, picked up the gun, shoved the gun in my pocket and flushed the glove down the toilet. It was then I heard the sirens. I was cut off. There was no escape. My car was parked in the alley. He had told me to come to the side door of the alley and go in the back part of the storeroom."

"You going to tell your story and disclose Gideon's connection with your wife?" Mason asked.

"I am not. I am going to keep tight-lipped."

"What did you do with the gun?"

"I'm a big clumsy boob, Mr. Mason. I had it in my pocket."

"You mean you kept it to protect your wife. You wanted to take the rap for her. Is it your gun?"

"Yes. I bought it. It's registered in my name."

Mason said, "All right. Don't tell anybody anything. Tell them that you are innocent of the murder, that you will tell the whole story when you are on the witness stand and not before. Don't give anyone so much as the time of day."

"What about Lorna? What will she say?"

"You leave Lorna to me," Mason said. "This is one hell of a murder case. They've got you boxed in. If they can find out anything about Lorna, they'll use that for motivation. What about Judson Olney, can you count on him to keep quiet?"

"I don't know. I hope so."

"I sure as hell hope so," Mason said. "But if the police start sweating him he'll crack and the fat will be in the fire."

Chapter Fifteen

MASON DIDN'T spare the time to get his car out of the parking lot. He hailed a taxicab, jumped in and said, "Get me to 2420 Bridamoore just as fast as you can make it."

"Hang on," the driver said. "I'll get you there fast."

"All right," Mason told him. "It's an emergency. There's a twenty-dollar tip for scaring me half to death."

The driver grinned, concentrated on traffic, whipping his car through every opening, racing for the signals.

As they turned into Bridamoore, Mason heaved a sigh of relief as he saw Della Street's car parked in front of the building but no police cars.

The lawyer tossed the taxi driver a twenty and a ten, said, "Keep the change. It was worth it. Thanks," and dashed for the house.

"Want me to wait?" the driver asked.

Mason waved his hand in a gesture of dismissal, tried the front door. It was open. The lawyer walked in.

"Hello, Della!" he called.

"This way, Chief," he heard Della's voice saying.

Mason ran through the reception hall, across the living room into a den.

Della Street was seated, with a tearful Lorna Warren regarding her hopelessly.

"Look," Mason said. "Look and listen. We haven't much time. Now, get this straight. Your husband has been arrested for the murder of Collister Gideon. They *may* not be able to make a case if he doesn't say anything and you don't say anything. They're going to have to prove motivation. Now, you're going to have to tell a fib. You're going to have to tell the officers that your husband asked you not to talk about anything, that it was absurd to think that he would be charged with murder, and that your best course was that of dignified silence.

"If the officers can ever prove that you knew Gideon, or ever worked with him, they'll have a motivation and—"

"Don't I have to answer questions?"

"You can't testify against your husband," Mason said. "Tell them that after they turn your husband loose you'll talk, but that while your husband is in custody you're not going to tell them one word."

"To think," she said tearfully, "that I thought this Gideon was such a gentleman. . . . Mr. Mason, the man turned out to be a monster. . . .

At one time he had me completely hypnotized. I thought he was one of the most wonderful men in the world, one of the most wonderful thinkers, a shrewd businessman, a gentleman, an idealist, a—"

"Save it," Mason said, as the doorbell rang. "That'll be Lieutenant Tragg. Remember now, if they ever get any suspicion of the truth, they'll prove motivation. I don't want that to happen. If they ask to take your fingerprints, tell them you'll only do it with my consent. Now, tell me, was he dead when you were there, or alive?"

"He was alive and terribly obnoxious."

"Did you take him forty-seven thousand dollars?"

"I took him five thousand dollars, which was all I could raise at the time."

"Did you take custody of the forty-seven thousand or— Hold it, hold it!" Mason said. "Here's Tragg now."

Tragg said, "The front door was unlocked so I came on in. Well hello, everybody. How are you, Mason? I rather expected to find you here. Rather fast work.

"I take it this is Mrs. Warren?"

"That's right," Mason said. "This is Mrs. Horace Warren. And for your information, Lieutenant, as long as her husband is in custody she doesn't have a word to say to officers."

"Why not?"

"Because," Mason said, "you wouldn't be interested in anything that was in favor of the

160

defendant and under the law she can't testify to anything against him."

"Tut-tut-tut," Tragg said. "That's quite a technicality. You know as well as I do, Mason, that we're just investigating the crime at this stage of the proceedings. If she can tell us anything in her husband's favor, we'll not only believe it but we'll act on it."

"She doesn't know a thing," Mason said.

"Well," Tragg said, "we *could* question her here and excuse you and Della Street, or we *can* take her to the district attorney's office."

"You can't take her anywhere without a warrant," Mason said, "and you can't force me to leave."

Tragg's eyes narrowed. "One would almost think that she knows something," he said.

"She knows how foolish you are to be trying to work up a case against her husband," Mason said. "I have just told her that her husband was arrested and charged with murder."

"Oh, leave it to you," Tragg said. "You'd tell her all right. You must have broken all speed laws getting here. We moved right along. I just had to have a few words with Horace Warren after you left him, to see if he was going to make any statements, and I had some chores to do at the scene of the crime.

"It would be a lot better for both Mr. and Mrs. Warren if they'd make a frank statement. I'm free to tell you, Mason, that as a veteran homicide investigator, they don't impress me as being the type that would be mixed up with murder. . . . Tell me, Mrs. Warren, have you been in the vicinity of Clovina and Hendersell Streets today?"

"She's making no comment," Mason said. "Mrs. Warren, I instruct you to say 'no comment' to any question that Lieutenant Tragg may ask you."

"Well now," Tragg said, "that looks very much as though she *had* been down there. That complicates the situation somewhat."

"No comment," Mrs. Warren said.

Tragg looked at her. "You're an apt pupil."

"No comment."

"Aren't you interested in saving your husband the publicity and the humiliation of being a defendant in a murder case?"

"No comment."

Mason grinned.

Tragg frowned and got to his feet. "All right, Mason," he said. "You win this round. This is only the opening part of the fight. We're feeling each other out. Later on I think you'll be on the ropes, fighting to keep on your feet. I think you're mixed in this pretty much yourself."

"No comment," Mason said.

Chapter Sixteen

PAUL DRAKE was waiting in Mason's office when the lawyer and Della returned.

Mason said, "For your information, Paul, Collister Gideon was murdered. Horace Warren has been charged with the crime. Neither Warren nor his wife is making any statement."

"I know, I know," Drake said. "That's *your* news. Wait until you hear mine."

"What's yours?" Mason asked.

"The artist that I had make the phony composite picture of Collister Gideon was up at headquarters. He showed the picture we had him make to someone on the homicide squad to see if it checked with anything they had.

"They were just fresh from investigating the Gideon murder and recognized the picture right away as a sketch of Gideon, so they wanted to know what had happened and who the artist had made it for, and why, and he referred them to me and I mean the police came down on me *hard*."

"You didn't do anything illegal," Mason said.

"The hell I didn't," Drake said. "There's a law about tampering with witnesses."

"What witnesses did you tamper with?" Mason asked.

"You know damned well how I tampered with them," Drake said. "I took the sketch along and tried to get the witnesses to describe the man in the sketch as having the same general appearance as that of the man they had seen running out of the place. The artist said he was under instructions to duplicate a picture of Gideon.

"This is too big for me to take by myself, Perry. They suspected what had happened anyway, so I finally told them that I was acting under orders and that you had given the orders."

"So what do they intend to do?" Mason asked.

"They intend to raise hell with you for lousing up a robbery case.

"They think that you were trying to protect a client, that you're representing the man who held up the supermarket and shot the watchman and that he hasn't been apprehended as yet, but that you're getting in and trying to confuse the witnesses. Hamilton Burger, the district attorney, is going to send for you and put you on the carpet. And he's going to release to the press exactly what happened."

"Let him release," Mason said. "I acted within my rights as a citizen. I wanted to know who held up that supermarket."

"Why?" Drake asked.

"That's none of their damned business,"

Mason said. "I don't have to account to them for my actions. I'm a licensed attorney at law. I can investigate any crime I damned please and do anything I want to, to protect the interests of my clients, just so I keep within the law. . . . And I sure as hell am going to protect my clients as long as I have any breath and pulse."

"You tried to influence those people in making an identification."

"The police do that a dozen times every twenty-four hours," Mason said. "They get a favorite suspect in a particular case, or they work with a mug shot and they force an identification. They say, 'Look at this picture, look at it good. Look at this mug shot. Now remember the man who held you up. Now look at this sketch by the artist. Doesn't that resemble the man? Think carefully now, because if you don't answer this question right a guilty man may go free to commit other crimes.'

"Don't tell me that it's a crime to ask a witness to identify a picture, because if it is every police officer in the country will be in jail."

"Well, I'm just letting you know," Drake said, "because—"

The telephone rang several short, sharp rings, Gertie's signal that there was some emergency in the outer office.

The office door opened and a young man entered, saying, "I'm Tarlton Ladd. I'm an investigator for the district attorney's office. Here are my credentials if you care to check them."

"Okay," Mason said, "you're an investigator for the D.A. What do you want?"

"The district attorney wants to interrogate you on a matter which may lead to the institution of criminal proceedings."

"Against whom?"

"You."

"When does he want to interrogate me?"

"Now."

"And if I don't choose to go?"

"Then I have a subpoena ordering you to appear before the grand jury tomorrow at ten o'clock."

Mason thought things over for a moment, then said, "Okay, I'll go."

Mason turned to Della Street. "You mind the store until I get back, Della."

Mason's last view of his office before the door clicked shut showed Della Street and Paul Drake standing silent with apprehensive faces.

Chapter Seventeen

HAMILTON BURGER, the district attorney, said, "This is in the nature of a formal hearing for the purpose of making a criminal complaint if the evidence indicates a crime has been committed, or preferring charges before the disciplinary division of the Bar Association, or both.

"Mr. Mason, you are acquainted with Sergeant Holcomb of the police department and this is Drummond Dixon, an artist, and Drew Kearny. The other gentleman is Farley Fulton, a private detective employed on occasion by the Drake Detective Agency and we have here a court reporter who is taking down the proceedings."

"Will I have a right to ask questions?" Mason asked.

"This is not a court hearing. We are trying to determine whether there is ground for taking action."

"Are you afraid to have these witnesses interrogated except by one side?"

"I'm not afraid of anything or anyone in

connection with an investigation of this sort."

"Very well, then I want to have the right to ask questions."

"I see no reason for you to be given an opportunity to cross-examine these witnesses."

"Then I'll get up and walk out," Mason said. "If you're going to conduct a star-chamber session and try to influence witnesses to testify your way, I'm not going to have anything to do with it."

"I'm not trying to influence witnesses and you know it," Hamilton Burger said angrily. "You've been guilty of some rather sharp practices at times."

"Sharp but legal," Mason said. "When I represent a client I try to represent him."

"Well, there's no use having all this bickering," Hamilton Burger said. "We'll proceed with the hearing and if you want to ask questions, you may ask them, but if the questions are not within the bounds of propriety I will advise the witness not to answer them."

"At which stage I'll get up and walk out," Mason said.

"Whereupon you'll be brought before the grand jury," Hamilton Burger warned.

"At which time I'll tell my side of the story, that you were having a star-chamber session, that I was willing to be present and answer questions but I wanted to have the matter fairly presented and to that end insisted on my right to ask questions."

"We'll start with Farley Fulton," Burger said. "What's your occupation, Mr. Fulton?"

"I'm a private detective."

"Early this month were you employed by anyone in such capacity?"

"I was."

"What person?"

"Paul Drake."

"That's the head of Drake Detective Agency?"

"Yes, sir."

"And what were you ordered to do by Mr. Drake?"

"I was given a photograph and told to have Mr. Dixon, whom I knew, practice making sketches from that photograph so that he could make a likeness in crayon."

"And what else were you told to do?"

"I was told to hunt up the eyewitnesses to the holdup at the Pacific and Northern Supermarket, the wounded watchman and Mr. Kearny here, and tell them I was investigating the crime which had taken place there, involving the attempted murder of the watchman. I was to ask them to give me a general description of what the holdup man had looked like. That was on the morning of the fourth.

"I was instructed to take the sketch made by my friend, Drummond Dixon, submit it to the witnesses and ask them if that didn't look like the man they had seen."

"What was the name of the man whose photograph you were given?"

169

"Collister Gideon."

"Do you know what has happened to Collister Gideon?"

"Yes, I do now. He was killed earlier today."

"Did you know anything about the background of Gideon?"

"I knew that he had been convicted of crime. I knew that the photograph from which we made up our spurious, synthetic 'composite' sketch was a police photogaph."

"All right, what did you do?"

"I carried out my instructions."

"Were you present when Mr. Dixon made the sketch?"

"I was."

"Is this a copy of the sketch?"

"It is."

"And you showed this to the witnesses?"

"Yes."

"And, in accordance with your instructions, did everything you could to get the witnesses to state that that was a reasonable likeness of the man they had seen who held up the Pacific and Northern Supermarket shortly after midnight on the night Steven Hooks was wounded?"

"Yes, sir."

"Are you familiar with the provisions of the Penal Code that any person who attempts fraudulently to induce any person to give false testimony is guilty of a felony?"

"Yes, sir."

"And that every person who knowingly makes

or exhibits any false writing or document to any witness with intent to affect the testimony of such witness is guilty of a crime?''

"Yes, sir."

"Yet your instructions were to get these two witnesses to identify the sketch of Collister Gideon as that of the man the watchman had seen, and the one Kearny had seen running from the supermarket?''

"If they would, yes, sir."

"I think that covers it," Hamilton Burger said.

"Just a moment," Mason said. "I'd like to ask some questions of this witness."

"Proper questions will be permitted," Hamilton Burger said.

Mason turned to Fulton. "Fulton," he asked, "were you instructed to bribe these witnesses?''

"Certainly not."

"To intimidate them?''

"No, sir."

"To make any false statements to them?''

"No, sir."

"You were simply to show that sketch to the witnesses and ask them if that was the man?''

"Well, it was a little more than that. I was told to do what I could to convince the witnesses that was the man they had seen."

"But not to bribe them?''

"No, sir."

"Not to make false statements to them?''

"No, sir."

"Not to intimidate them."

"No, sir."

"That's all," Mason said.

Hamilton Burger said, "All right, Mr. Kearny, I'm going to ask *you* about what happened. You had an interview with Mr. Fulton, the detective who has just made a statement?"

"Yes, sir. I also had an interview with Paul Drake and with Mr. Mason, here."

"And you were asked to describe the man you had seen running from the supermarket?"

"Yes, sir."

"Did you describe him?"

"Yes, sir."

"Did you identify the sketch?"

"Hell, no!"

"Tell me what happened?"

"Well, right away Fulton started saying to me, 'Now, that's the man, isn't it? That picture answers your description.' "

"He kept suggesting to you that was the man?"

"Yes."

"And what did you do?"

"I said it wasn't the man."

"And you went to Paul Drake's office?"

"Yes, sir."

"What happened?"

"He took me to Mason's office. Mason wasn't quite as bad as the others, but he tried to get me to say this fellow in the sketch was the one I had seen running out of the building."

"Did you do it?"

"No, after a while they got me sort of confused

172

and I said there was something familiar about the eyes, but the mouth was all wrong.

"To tell the truth, they got me so confused I can't remember where the face I saw leaves off and this face in the sketch begins."

"You feel your ability to be a truthful witness has been impaired?"

"Yes."

"That's all," Hamilton Burger said.

"Just a minute," Mason said. "I have some questions."

"I don't think I will permit you to examine this witness, Mr. Mason," Burger said.

Kearny said, "Don't get me wrong. I don't want to accuse anyone of any crime. I just can't be certain to what extent my memory has been impaired by the suggestions that have been made to me, that's all."

Hamilton Burger said, "There you are. That covers the situation. The testimony of this eyewitness has been ruined as far as any successful prosecution is concerned.

"When we get the real culprit and this witness is confronted with the man who really committed the crime, he will have to admit on cross-examination that he has previously made statements that would detract from his identification due to improper inducements made by Perry Mason and by persons in the employ of Mr. Perry Mason."

Mason said, "In just about every prosecution that you have, the witnesses first give

173

contradictory descriptions to the police. Then they have to back up and when they finally make an identification it's very likely to have been the second identification they have made. That's why the police refer to identifications from line-ups so many times as 'tentative' identifications.''

"That's neither here nor there," Hamilton Burger said. "The gist of the offense, as I see it, is that the testimony of this witness has been tampered with."

"The testimony hasn't been tampered with," Mason said. "What you're trying to state is that the mind of the witness has been tampered with."

"It's the same thing," Hamilton Burger said.

"Take it into court and see if it's the same thing," Mason said.

Hamilton Burger said, "I don't care to prolong this examination or add to the record."

Mason said, "The police usually show a witness composite sketches and mug shots, and after they've given him an opportunity to look at a photograph of a suspect under all kinds of circumstances they then let him look at a line-up containing the suspect."

"That will do," Hamilton Burger said. "We're not here to discuss police methods."

"I am," Mason said.

"I am not," Hamilton Burger said, "and the hearing is terminated. As far as this office is concerned, I think I will lodge a complaint with the authorities concerning the improper activities of a private detective and lodge a complaint with the disciplinary section of the Bar Association about your activities."

Mason said, "You've been brandishing a couple of sections of the Penal Code around, Mr. District Attorney. Now, if you think you've got any violation of the Penal Code you just go ahead and issue a warrant for my arrest and bring me to trial before a jury. Then I'll cross-examine these witnesses, and you can't ask them all these leading questions. Then we'll see how much of a case you've got."

Hamilton Burger said, "I am going to do that very thing."

"Go right ahead," Mason invited.

Mason got up and stalked out of the room.

Chapter Eighteen

PERRY MASON sat in the living room at the residence at 2420 Bridamoore Avenue.

Mrs. Horace Warren sat facing him. She was dry-eyed but crushed.

Mason said, "We may not have much time. I want you to tell me exactly what happened. I want you to tell me your connection with Collister Gideon and tell me what happened when you went to that abandoned storeroom. Don't leave out anything, don't spare yourself."

"This is going to kill me," she said. "I can't face Horace after this comes out."

"Don't be silly," Mason said. "Horace has faith in you."

"He won't after this."

"He has," Mason said. "He knew all about it before he married you."

Her eyes widened. "Knew about what?"

"About your trial and acquittal, about your connection with Collister Gideon."

"He knew about *that?*"

176

"Yes."

"For heaven's sake, how?"

"Judson Olney backtracked you and found out all about your past. When Horace knew that he was falling in love with you, he knew that you were concealing something in your past and he wanted to find out what it was."

"And he never told me?"

"He thought you would feel better if you felt the whole thing was a secret."

"You're not trying to make things easier for me, Mr. Mason?"

"I'm telling you the truth," Mason said.

"Oh, that wonderful, wonderful man," she said, and tears came to her eyes.

"Hold it," Mason said. "You haven't time to cry, you haven't time to sympathize with yourself."

"I'm not sympathizing with myself, I'm thinking of Horace, how wonderful he has been."

"All right," Mason said, "he's been wonderful. Now tell me the facts. That's the best way you can co-operate with him at present."

She said, "I always felt morally obligated to Collister Gideon for forty-seven thousand dollars."

"Did you keep the money for him?"

"Heavens, no."

"What did happen?"

"He had an inkling that the authorities might be coming down on him in a surprise raid. There was forty-seven thousand dollars in the bank. He

177

drew it out and put it in the safe. He wanted me to keep it for him. I was afraid to do so. I knew that there were certain irregularities but I looked up to Mr. Gideon. I thought he was the most wonderful, wide-awake businessman, with a dynamic personality and . . . well, it just never occurred to me he could be crooked.

"He put the forty-seven thousand dollars in the safe and told me to take it out and hide it. I didn't do it. That night the office was broken into, the thieves found the combination of the safe, and took the forty-seven thousand dollars."

"If he'd had it," Mason said, "the authorities would have confiscated it as being obtained by fraudulent use of the mails."

"They might have had some difficulty proving it, but anyway I didn't follow the instructions he gave me. I was afraid to, and as a result he lost all chance of holding onto any part of the forty-seven thousand dollars."

"So when you knew he was getting out," Mason said, "you thought you would make restitution?"

She said, "My husband has been very, very successful in business, and I have been saving money here and there in securities and looking forward to the day when Collister Gideon would be released. I wanted to go to him and say, 'I violated your instructions and because of that you lost any opportunity to have operating capital when you got out. I'm going to stake you to forty-seven thousand dollars. I know that with your talents for making money you will run this up into quite a fortune within a short time. Then you can pay me back the forty-seven thousand dollars and my husband will never know anything about it.' "

"Go on," Mason said, "what happened?"

"I put the money in a suitcase in my closet and the money was stolen. One of the servants, probably. But I wasn't in a position to make a complaint because that would have brought out the whole scandal and that would have— Well, I felt Horace simply couldn't stand to be connected with a scandal of that sort. He likes his social position and his social life."

"All right," Mason said, "the money you had in the suitcase was stolen. Then what did you do?"

"I got together what I could raise hastily, which amounted to only five-thousand dollars."

"You heard from Gideon?"

"Yes. He telephoned me and gave me the address of the store and told me to drive down there.

"I told him that I had some money for him and he said the neighborhood was pretty rough. He asked me if I had a revolver and I told him I did; that is, I told him my husband kept one in the house and he said if I was bringing any large sum of money I had better bring the gun to protect myself."

"Go on," Mason said.

"I went down there and found the place

without any trouble. I had the gun in my handbag. I went into the abandoned store and saw Collister Gideon. I was startled at the change in him.

"I took off my right glove, opened my purse to give him the money, put the gun on the table, and— Well, I don't know, Mr. Mason, whether *he* had changed or whether *I* had begun to grow up.

"While I was working for him I saw him as a dynamic, magnetic businessman with a chain-lightning mind. But as I talked with him there in the store I saw him as a brazen, glib-tongued confidence man. There wasn't an ounce of sincerity in him, and . . . well, he sought to capitalize on the relationship."

"What do you mean?"

"He knew that I had looked up to him and idolized him when I was working for him and . . . well, he thought that he could twist me around his finger and— Well, it was just one of those things."

"What did you do?"

She said, "Suddenly I saw the whole thing in its real perspective. It was a disgusting situation. I simply grabbed my handbag and dashed out of the place."

"What about the gun?"

"I left it on the table. My right glove was on the floor, I guess. I didn't see it. To tell the truth, I wasn't thinking. I was simply reacting. I was getting out of there as fast as I could."

"He was alive when you left?"

"Of course. He was very much alive."

"Do you know what time it was?"

"I know that he told me to be there at quarter past two and I was there right on the dot. We talked for only a minute or two. The situation became unbearable with considerable rapidity —unbearable as far as I was concerned.

"It's difficult to keep track of time in a situation of that sort, Mr. Mason. . . . They say he was killed with my gun."

"Apparently so," Mason said, "but they haven't introduced proof of it yet, and when they do I'm going to have the right of cross-examination."

"But that was the only gun in the place."

"If your husband shot him," Mason said, "he might well have been shot with your gun, but your husband tells me he didn't shoot him."

"My husband wouldn't lie about such things."

"In a murder case many times things are entirely different from what they are in other cases," Mason said. "When a man's life is at stake he will do almost anything."

Mrs. Warren blinked back the tears. "Do you really mean his life is at stake?"

"Yes," Mason said.

"And it's . . . it's my fault," she said, "I—"

Mason said, "Make up your mind to one thing, Mrs. Warren. After water has run downstream and over the dam you can't find any way on earth of getting it back upstream and over the dam the second time. Take things as they

181

come. Concentrate on the present, forget the past. . . . You didn't give Gideon any money?"

"Not a cent."

"Did you tell him you had some money for him?"

"Yes. That was over the phone. I told him I had some money for him, not as much as I'd hoped to have, but all I could raise without attracting attention. I started talking and telling him how sorry I was that I hadn't followed his instructions to get that money out of the safe and conceal it, but I pointed out that if they had found the money in my possession that would have been bad and— And then when I met him, Mr. Mason, I suddenly saw a look in his eye that made me think that perhaps he had hoped he could get me so completely involved in the case with him that the jury would have become sympathetic and acquitted both of us.

"As it was, the cases against us were so sharply different that the jury was able to acquit me and still convict him, but if the cases had been mixed up a little closer— I don't know. I just suddenly lost my feeling of awed admiration for the man and saw him as a tawdry performer."

Mason said, "You don't know how long you talked."

"Just a minute or two."

"And he didn't tell you anything about what he had been doing since he got out?"

"No."

"You had only the one telephone call from

Gideon?" Mason asked.

"That's right. I hadn't heard from him directly from the time he was convicted and went to prison until after he got out and made that one phone call to me. I'll say that, he was considerate of me. He didn't want any publicity to involve me."

"Sure he didn't," Mason said, "because he wanted to blackmail your husband."

"He wanted . . . *what?*"

"He wanted to blackmail your husband," Mason said. "That was one of the things he had in mind. He—"

"Oh, but he wouldn't have done anything like that. He wouldn't have been that low."

"Don't kid yourself," Mason said. "He came to my office and tried to get me to finance him by getting your husband to put in money to avoid the publicity."

Her mouth sagged open. "Why . . . why—Well, of all things!"

"You had no idea of that?"

"No."

"All right," Mason said. "You've told me about your background and about what happened when you got into that storeroom. Now, don't tell anyone else. Make absolutely no comment to anybody about anything."

"But it will all have to come out now," she said. "My association with Gideon and—"

"No, it won't," Mason said. "Not necessarily. I'm going to put up a fight. I'm forcing the state to an immediate preliminary examination and we'll see just how much of a case they've got against your husband."

"I'm afraid it's a perfectly devastating case," she said, "even if they don't know everything about the background."

"They won't necessarily try to prove motivation at a preliminary hearing," Mason said. "Where did you get the gun?"

"My husband got it."

"Where? When?"

"He bought it several years ago."

"From a friend or from a firearms dealer?"

"I believe from a firearms dealer. He wanted a gun to keep in the house."

"All right," Mason said, "we'll do the best we can. You sit tight and make absolutely no comment about anything. As far as possible adopt the position that you are too prostrated to submit to interviews. Don't let any newspapermen in the house, don't answer the telephone yourself, and if you should be cornered by any person who wants an interview, don't let that person trap you into making any statement of any sort other than the two words 'no comment.' Use those words whenever you open your mouth. Think you can do that?"

"Yes, of course."

"It's not going to be as easy as you think," Mason said. "They'll suddenly throw questions at you or make definite assertions of things that aren't true and try to catch you by surprise.

Simply remember and say 'no comment' and keep saying 'no comment.' In that way you can help your husband. Otherwise you may inadvertently hurt him.''

''I'll try,'' she said.

Chapter Nineteen

JUDGE ROMNEY Saxton took his position on the bench and said, "The case of the People of the State of California versus Horace Warren. This is a preliminary examination for murder. Is the case ready to be heard?"

"Ready for the defense," Perry Mason said.

Hamilton Burger got to his feet. "If the Court please, in announcing that we are ready for the prosecution I wish to state that my trial deputy, Alpheus Randolph, will assist me in presenting the case.

"I am aware that an opening statement is not usually made in connection with a preliminary hearing. I am also aware my personal appearance in a preliminary examination is highly unusual, but this is an unusual case. Because of the peculiar circumstances surrounding this hearing, I desire to make a statement to the Court so that the Court will understand the purpose of the evidence we are introducing and how it fits into an over-all pattern.

"We have, for instance, been unable to find a motivation for murder in the evidence in this case except by implication and by circumstantial evidence.

"We propose to introduce that circumstantial evidence and let the Court draw its own conclusions.

"We shall be able to show that on the night of the third of this month an attempted murder was committed in connection with the holdup of the main branch of the Pacific Northern Supermarket in this city. There were two witnesses who saw the murderer.

"Mr. Perry Mason, who is the attorney for the defendant in this case, employed an artist to make a sketch of the decedent; this was done in advance of any interview with those witnesses and before hearing any description given by those witnesses.

"The circumstantial evidence indicated conclusively that Mr. Mason intended to use this to exert pressure to bear on the decedent, Collister Gideon.

"Gideon had been convicted of a felony previously and had but recently been released from the federal prison. Knowing that a person of Mr. Mason's influence was intending to frame an attempted murder charge on him, he could conceivably have been expected to panic."

"Now, just a minute," Judge Saxton interrupted, "This is a serious charge. Are you intimating that Mr. Mason was framing an attempted murder case on the decedent?"

"That is what I said, Your Honor."

"And that he tampered with the testimony of witnesses?"

"That is my charge and I expect to prove it by way of motivation."

"That is a most serious charge," Judge Saxton said.

"The proof will substantiate the charge," Hamilton Burger asserted.

Judge Saxton's mouth set in a grim line. "Very well," he said. "Proceed with your statement."

"We will prove," Hamilton Burger went on, "that the decedent, Collister Gideon, was killed by a thirty-eight-caliber revolver which was found in the possession of the defendant, that the defendant was found hiding at the scene of the murder. On the strength of that evidence we will ask for an order binding the defendant over to the Superior Court for trial."

"Very well," Judge Saxton said. "Does the defense wish to make an opening statement?"

Perry Mason got to his feet. "The defense wishes to make this statement: The defendant is presumed innocent until he is proven guilty. I am presumed innocent until I have been proven guilty.

"The defense would like to have the Court keep in mind that any suggestion made to a witness is not necessarily an unlawful attempt to get a witness to falsify his testimony."

"I don't think you need to worry about this Court understanding the fundamentals of criminal law, Mr. Mason. The People will proceed."

Hamilton Burger said, "If the Court please, under the unusual circumstances of this case, I am going to call Mr. Drew Kearny as my first witness because I want to lay the foundation for showing the motivation in this case."

"Do I understand Mr. Kearny's testimony goes to motivation?"

"Yes, Your Honor."

"In what way?"

"We propose to show that the defendant, through his attorney, Perry Mason, was trying to frame an attempted murder charge on Collister Gideon, the decedent in this case."

"The Court is very much interested in that evidence," Judge Saxton said. "Mr. Drew Kearny will come forward and be sworn."

Kearny came forward, held up his right hand, was sworn, gave his name, address, his occupation.

"You have a store in this city?"

"A small store, yes sir. I have a store and shop combined. I do electrical repair work and sell some electrical goods."

"Now, do you have occasion to remember the third of this month?"

"I do, yes, sir."

"Where were you on that date?"

"Well, actually it was just a few minutes past midnight so I suppose technically it was on the morning of the fourth," Kearny said. "I had been to a late movie and was walking home."

"Are you familiar with the location of the Pacific Northern Supermarket at 1026 Hallston Avenue?"

"I am, yes, sir."

"Did your route take you past that supermarket?"

"It did. Yes, sir."

"While you were there did anything unusual happen?"

"Yes, sir."

"What?"

"The front door of the market opened, a man came running out and almost collided with me."

"Then what happened?"

"This man held a revolver in his hand. He put the revolver in front of me and told me to put up my hands."

"What did you do?"

"I put up my hands."

"Did the man make any other statements?"

"I had assumed it was a holdup and—"

"Never mind what you had assumed. The question is: Did the man make any other statements?"

"Yes, sir."

"What did he say?"

"He said, 'Keep them up.' "

"Then what did he do?"

"He started backing away from me, moving rather rapidly backwards until he was nearly two-thirds of the way across the street. Then he

190

suddenly turned and ran as fast as he could down the alley.''

"What did you do?"

"I tried the door of the store. It was locked. There was a spring lock on the inside, but I sensed something was wrong and I started for a telephone. I wanted to get there as fast as I could and notify the police.''

"You were familiar with the neighborhood?"

"Yes, sir."

"Did you know where the nearest telephone was located?"

"Well now, I'm not certain that it was the *nearest* telephone but I knew there was a telephone booth at a service station about three blocks down the street, so I started running.''

"How fast were you running?"

The witness grinned. "As fast as I could at the start, but I slowed down pretty quick. I used to do some sprinting but I found out I was pretty badly out of shape. I slowed down to a jog-trot after a couple of blocks and then I heard the siren and saw the red light of this police car coming, so I ran out in the middle of the street, waved my hands and flagged it down.''

"All right, we'll pass up what happened after that for the moment," Burger said, "and go on to what happened later on."

"Well, you mean about the sketch?"

"Yes."

"Well, a man whose name was Farley Fulton came to call on me. He had a sketch, a pencil sketch, and he showed it to me and asked me if that was the man I had seen. . . . Well now, wait a minute. There was some conversation before that. First he asked me generally to describe the man I'd seen. He told me he was a private detective and showed me his credentials, and then he showed me this sketch and asked me if that wasn't a picture of the man I had seen and if the physical description wasn't a match."

"What did you tell him?"

"I looked at the sketch and told him no, that wasn't the man."

"Then what happened?"

"Well, he became rather insistent. He told me that there was no question about it, that was the man; that the night watchman had said it was a perfect likeness."

"Then what happened?"

"Well, I told him I didn't think so, but I got worrying about it, thinking about it. Frankly it bothered me a lot. I'd been held up before and I didn't want—"

"Now, never mind that. Never mind your thoughts or your background," Hamilton Burger interrupted. "Just what did you do?"

"Well, I went to the office of Paul Drake, the detective who employed Farley Fulton, and I asked him if I could see that sketch again. Well, he put through a telephone call to Mr. Mason and asked him—"

"Now, just a minute," Hamilton Burger interrupted, "when you say Mr. Mason, you mean Mr. Perry Mason, the attorney representing the defense in this case?"

"That's the one. Yes, sir."

"And what happened?"

"Well, he called Mr. Mason, and Mason had us come down to his office and when we got down there Mason talked with me himself."

"And what was the tenor of Mason's conversation?"

"Objected to as calling for a conclusion of the witness," Mason said.

"Sustained," Judge Saxton snapped.

"Well, what did Mason say to you?"

"Well, I can't remember all that he said, but I remember he showed me the picture and I told him that the man I had seen was older and heavier and taller, and he told me that experience showed that under such circumstances witnesses almost invariably described the man as being older and heavier and taller and more powerfully built than the actual criminal."

"In other words, he was trying to get you to identify this sketch?"

"Just a moment, Your Honor," Mason said, "I object to the question as leading and suggestive, and calling for a conclusion of the witness."

"Sustained," Judge Saxton said. "Mr. District Attorney, in a matter of this importance kindly refrain from asking leading questions."

"Well, I think it was obvious what was happening," Hamilton Burger said. "I was simply trying to summarize the situation."

"Just let the evidence come in by question and answer," Judge Saxton said, "and there will be no need to summarize the situation."

"At any time did Mr. Mason ask you to identify this sketch?"

"Well, I can't remember exactly that he said those exact words. I know what he was trying to get me to do, but—"

"Move to strike out the answer as not being responsive to the question," Mason interposed.

"Sustained. Motion granted."

"Did Mr. Mason at any time ask you to identify this sketch?"

"I thought he did. I was certain that's what he was trying to get me to do."

"Move to strike out the answer as not being responsive and being a conclusion of the witness," Mason said.

"Motion granted."

"Well," Hamilton Burger said, "getting back to your own mind now. Did your conversation with Mason raise any doubt in your mind as to the identity of the man you had seen?"

"It did."

"In what way?"

"Well, I thought I knew what the man looked like pretty well, but after I'd seen that sketch half a dozen times and after they'd talked with me about it, I began to get a little dubious."

"Did you say anything to Mr. Mason which indicated such was the case?"

"I told him that there was something wrong with the picture of the fellow's mouth but that the eyes were beginning to look a little familiar. They looked like somebody I had seen somewhere."

"And what did Mr. Mason say with reference to that statement?"

"He seemed quite gratified."

"Never mind what he *seemed*," Hamilton Burger said. "I'm asking you what he said."

"Well, he told me that it was very important to get the right man and that I was to search my recollection and do the best I could."

Hamilton Burger looked at Perry Mason. "We can stipulate that that sketch was one of Collister Gideon, Mr. Mason?"

"We can stipulate nothing of the sort," Mason said. "If you want to prove your case, go ahead and prove it."

"If I have to, I can put the artist on the stand and show that he made the sketch from a picture of Collister Gideon and that in doing so he was acting under instructions."

"And how are you going to show that was the same sketch that was exhibited to this witness?"

"Oh," Hamilton Burger said irritably, "if you want to drag this thing out in a last-ditch fight, go ahead. Actually I have a photographic copy of the original sketch made by the artist in my office."

"That's not the one that was shown to the witness here," Mason said.

Judge Saxton said, "Well, I can appreciate, in a matter of this importance, counsel wants to protect his rights. Why don't you excuse this witness, get the artist to produce a copy of the sketch and bring it here this afternoon?"

"I'll do that," Hamilton Burger said, "but I'd like to tie up the testimony of the witness."

He turned to Kearny. "Did you subsequently see a photograph of Collister Gideon?"

"Yes, sir."

"And was this sketch that Mr. Mason's detective, Farley Fulton, showed you a likeness of Collister Gideon?"

"Just a moment," Mason said. "Let's get this thing in its proper sequence. That question calls for a conclusion of the witness, and furthermore you can't ask that question unless you can first show how he knows the picture he saw was that of Collister Gideon. If his knowledge was based on hearsay statements, you cannot connect the picture up in that way."

Hamilton Burger made a gesture of surrender. "All right," he said, "all right, all right. If the Court please, I ask to withdraw this witness until this afternoon and substitute Lieutenant Tragg."

"Just a moment," Judge Saxton said. "The Court would like to ask this witness a few questions."

Kearny looked up at Judge Saxton.

"You were interrogated by the police about what you had seen on the night of the third and the early morning of the fourth?"

"Yes, sir."

"And I suppose that by the time the morning

papers came out you knew the nature of the crime that had been committed?"

"Yes, Your Honor."

"And you read those papers?"

"Yes, sir."

"In other words," Judge Saxton said, "you didn't get very much sleep that night."

"I didn't get to bed until about three-thirty."

"And then this detective showed you this picture?"

"Yes, sir."

"Did he say anything about the picture when he showed it to you?"

"I think he said that it was a composite sketch made by a police artist."

Judge Saxton's face was grim. "I think," he said, "we'll let this witness go until this afternoon and you may call your next witness."

"We call Lieutenant Tragg," Hamilton Burger said.

Lt. Tragg came forward and was sworn, testified as to his name, address, occupation, and the fact that he had been a police lieutenant in the department of homicide for some years.

"On the fourth of this month did you have occasion to go to a deserted storeroom at the corner of Clovina Avenue and Hendersell in this city?"

"I did."

"What was the occasion of your making such a trip?"

"Someone had turned in a fire alarm. There

had been no fire, but the fire department had found a body in the building and had reported accordingly, and as a result I made a trip."

"What did you find?"

"I found the body of a man whom we subsequently identified as Collister D. Gideon, dead apparently from a gunshot wound, in a section of the storeroom which had evidently been fitted up as surreptitious living quarters. There were cases of canned goods, cooking utensils, a small solid-fuel stove, pans, and eating utensils. There were towels, soap, and other housekeeping facilities."

"Was water on in the building?"

"Yes, sir. Water was on in the building. It was connected to a large sink and also to a toilet."

"What else can you tell us about this building?"

"In back of the storeroom and as a part of the property, was a fairly large warehouse building."

"Was this filled with merchandise?"

"No, sir. Not with merchandise, but there was a large number of empty cardboard cartons, some of them quite large. These had not been hauled away but were stacked in several piles in the warehouse."

"And did you search this warehouse?"

"Yes, sir."

"What did you find?"

"We found the defendant hiding behind one of the piles of cartons. He was carrying a revolver in his hip pocket."

"Did he state what he was doing there?"

"He stated that he had been trapped by the fire apparatus, that he had heard the sirens and mistaken them for the police and had secreted himself and been unable to get out of the building before we found him."

"Did he make any further statement as to what he was doing there?"

"No, sir. At about that time Mr. Perry Mason, his attorney, advised him to answer all statements with the words, 'No comment.' "

"Did he make any further statements after that?"

"Only the words, 'No comment.' "

"Did you establish the ownership of the revolver?"

"Yes, sir. The revolver was purchased by the defendant himself. I have here a certified copy of the purchase sheet from the firearms register."

"May I have it, please?"

Lt. Tragg handed the sheet to Hamilton Burger.

"We ask that this be introduced in evidence," Hamilton Burger said.

"No objection," Mason said, "provided it is established that this is the weapon which fired the fatal bullet."

"We expect to establish that," Hamilton Burger said.

"I want it established before any evidence about the weapon is received," Mason said. "We are entitled to have the case presented in proper order. If this weapon did not fire the fatal shot, then any evidence concerning it is incompetent, irrelevant and immaterial."

"If that is the position taken by defense counsel," Hamilton Burger said, "I would like to withdraw this witness temporarily from the stand and ask Alexander Redfield, the county firearms expert, to take the stand."

"No objection," Mason said. "In fact that is, I believe, the proper procedure."

Alexander Redfield took the stand, listed his professional qualifications, and then turned to Hamilton Burger expectantly.

"I show you a Smith and Wesson revolver which has previously been marked for identification," Hamilton Burger said, "and ask you if you have fired test bullets from that revolver."

"I have."

"I ask you whether you were present at an autopsy when the fatal bullet was recovered from the body of Collister Gideon."

"I was."

"What happened to that bullet?"

"I took charge of it."

"Where is it now?"

"I have it."

"Will you give it to me, please?"

Redfield handed over the bullet.

"You are prepared to state this is the bullet which was removed from the body of Collister Gideon in your presence?"

"Yes, sir."

"I ask that it be introduced in evidence,"

Hamilton Burger said.

Mason said, "May I see it, please?"

He walked over and stood for some time studying the bullet, then he said, "No objection, Your Honor. It may be received in evidence."

"Now then," Hamilton Burger said, "I will ask you, Mr. Redfield, if in your opinion as an expert on firearms, this fatal bullet was fired from this weapon which I now hold in my hand, this Smith and Wesson revolver."

Redfield shifted his position slightly. "I have carefully examined the fatal bullet and compared it with the test bullets fired from this weapon. I have found many points of similarity."

"Predicating your answer upon your experience in the field and your knowledge of the science of ballistics, would you say that this fatal bullet was fired from this gun marked for identification, People's Exhibit B?"

"I would say that in all human probability, considering all the factors, the fatal bullet had been fired from that gun."

"Have you been able to find any indications in your microscopic examination of the fatal bullet which indicate it had *not* been fired from the gun, People's Exhibit B?"

"No, sir."

"Cross-examine," Burger said, triumphantly.

Mason walked up to face Redfield, who again shifted his position slightly.

"Mr. Redfield," Mason said, "I have the

highest regard for your qualifications and your integrity."

"Thank you, sir."

"I have had you as a witness in many cases, and I have had the opportunity to cross-examine you on occasion."

"Yes, sir."

"But I have never heard you make quite those answers," Mason said. "You state that you have not been able to find any indication that the fatal bullet was not fired from the gun, People's Exhibit B. You state that you found several marks of similarity and you state that in all human probability in your opinion considering *all* the factors, the bullet was fired from that gun."

"Yes, sir."

"Now, those are very peculiar answers. Somewhat different from the answers you ordinarily make. Have you carefully rehearsed those answers?"

"Well . . ." Redfield said, and hesitated.

"Go ahead," Mason said, "you're under oath."

"In all my cases," Redfield said, "since I am in the employ of the police department, I find it necessary to discuss what my testimony is going to be. That is, I make a report and then I'm usually questioned on that report."

"I understand," Mason said. "My question in this case was whether or not your answers had been very carefully rehearsed."

"Well, I discussed the matter with the district

attorney and told him what I could swear to and what I couldn't swear to."

"I'm asking you," Mason said, "if those answers were very carefully rehearsed."

"Well, I told the district attorney what my answers would be."

"And he suggested certain changes which you could, in good faith, make?"

"Not changes."

"Changes in the wording?"

"In the wording, yes."

"And wasn't the final suggestion made by the district attorney that he would ask you if, considering *all* the circumstances, you consider that in all human probability the fatal bullet had been fired from that gun?"

"Well, yes, he did suggest that, I believe."

"This fatal bullet," Mason said, "is pretty badly flattened?"

"Yes, sir."

"You can see the marks of what are known as the class characteristics on it?"

"Yes, sir."

"Those class characteristics relate to caliber, pitch of the lands and number of the lands?"

"Yes, sir."

"In other words, any bullet fired from a Smith and Wesson revolver made during the year when this gun was made would have those same class characteristics?"

"Yes, sir."

"Now the individual characteristics, the

striations are much more difficult to trace on this fatal bullet than is ordinarily the case?"

"That is right."

"Now, when you state that when you consider *all* the circumstances you consider that in all human probability the fatal bullet was fired from that revolver, People's Exhibit B, you are taking into consideration certain circumstances which are not entirely within the province of a ballistics expert."

"Well, that depends on what you mean."

"You are taking into consideration certain nontechnical factors?"

"Well, I suppose so, yes."

"You are taking into consideration the fact that the gun was found in the possession of a man who was hiding near the scene of the murder?"

"Yes, sir, I am."

"In other words, if this gun, People's Exhibit B, had come to you cold—that is, if it had been picked up in a pawn shop somewhere and the district attorney had said to you, 'Can you positively swear as a matter of ballistics evidence that this fatal bullet was fired from this gun?'—what would your answer be?"

Redfield hesitated, fidgeted, looked at the district attorney, said, "Well, under those circumstances, I would have to state that while it was apparent the bullet had been fired from a gun of the same make, I couldn't swear positively, basing my testimony solely on the science of ballistics, that the fatal bullet had been fired from this gun."

"And," Mason said, "now if you leave out certain circumstances which influence your opinion simply as a layman and predicate your testimony entirely on what you have found as an expert, you are again forced to admit that you can't tell positively that this fatal bullet was fired from this gun."

"That is right, yes, sir."

"That's all," Mason said.

"Now, as I understand it, if the Court please, Lieutenant Tragg was on the stand and I am to have an opportunity to cross-examine him."

"If the district attorney is finished."

"I have no further questions," Burger said.

"I have, however, about concluded my case. I am now going to ask the Court for an order directed to Mr. Perry Mason ordering him to appear in person this afternoon to show cause why he shouldn't be found guilty of contempt in tampering with the evidence of witnesses."

Judge Saxton said, "It is approaching the hour of the noon adjournment. If Mr. Mason's examination is brief, I think he can probably finish his cross-examination before noon. I believe that I will at that time make an order ordering Mr. Mason to appear in court at two-thirty this afternoon and show cause, if any he has, why he shouldn't be cited for contempt.

"The Court takes a very grave view of this attempt to influence the witnesses, but, on the other hand, the Court points out to the district attorney that the action may not be in contempt but may be a criminal action, and, of course, a disciplinary action before the Bar Association."

"Yes. Your Honor, I am aware of that," Hamilton Burger said. "But I think, since this witness was one who was actually called before this Court, and since it now appears that he has been influenced, his testimony tampered with, and the witness deceived, the Court has power to issue a citation for contempt."

"We'll argue the matter at two-thirty," Judge Saxton said.

"The witness wasn't deceived," Mason said. "He was interrogated."

"Interrogated in such a manner that his mind was made up for him," Hamilton Burger snapped.

"We'll go into that at two-thirty," Judge Saxton said.

"Lieutenant Tragg, will you return to the stand, please, for cross-examination by Mr. Mason?"

Lt. Tragg returned to the witness stand, seating himself comfortably in the manner of a veteran witness who has faced cross-examination many times in his life, is telling the truth and has nothing to fear.

Mason said, "Lieutenant Tragg, when your men arrived at this storeroom at the corner of Clovina and Hendersell, you found a body?"

"That is right."

"And you went through your usual procedure in connection with that body. You took photographs of the position of the body. You marked the outline in chalk on the floor. You searched the place?"

"Yes, sir."

"And you found the defendant?"

"Yes, sir. Hiding behind a pile of boxes."

"You say he was hiding. You mean that he was concealed?"

"Well, he was hiding. He was shrinking into the shadows."

"Into the shadows, Lieutenant?"

"That's what I said."

"Then the place was not well lighted?"

"The place was definitely not well lit. The utilities were only partially in service. The water in the storeroom was still on, but the electricity had been disconnected."

"That is rather a long, rambling building?"

"That is an old brick building."

"What about the illumination?"

"When the electricity is on, the front room, the storeroom where the body was found, can be well illuminated. The warehouse part was not so well illuminated. However, with the electricity off the whole place was gloomy and poorly lit. One had to wait until one's eyes accustomed themselves to semidarkness before being able to see things at all clearly in the warehouse."

"And that's where the defendant was found?"

"That's where he was hiding, yes, sir."

"Now, where was the gun?"

"The gun was in the defendant's pocket."

"It had been fired?"

"It had been recently fired."

"Your test determined that?"

"Yes."

"The gun was fully loaded?"

"Except for the one discharged cartridge."

"Did you go to the trouble of having the electricity turned on?" Mason asked.

Tragg smiled, "No, sir, we didn't have the electricity turned on. That would have required a deposit and a certain amount of delay."

"Yet you say that you searched the place?"

"We searched it."

"How well did you search it?"

"We found what we wanted."

"Which was what?"

"The murderer and the murder weapon."

"You assumed that the defendant was the murderer because he was hiding?"

"And because he had the murder weapon in his possession."

"Yet you have just heard the testimony of the ballistics expert in which he assumes that the weapon was the murder weapon in part because it was in the possession of the man you have branded as the murderer."

"That is a logical deduction," Lt. Tragg said. "However, there were other identifying marks indicating the revolver, People's Exhibit B, was the murder weapon."

"Did you take any lights into the warehouse?"

"No, sir."

"You just looked through it, found the defendant and took him into custody?"

"Yes, sir."

"For all you know someone else could have been hiding in that warehouse?"

"No, sir, we searched it well enough to know no one else was hiding."

"There were numerous large cardboard cartons in there, I believe you said?"

"Yes, sir."

"Some of them were big enough to hold a man?"

"Oh, I presume so, yes."

"You didn't move them. You didn't look inside them?"

"No, we didn't. We made a search for the purpose of finding anyone who might be in there. We found the murderer. That terminated our search."

"Then," Mason said, "you haven't really searched the place. I am going to put up the money for connecting the electric light service and I suggest that this case be continued until a search can be made."

"What do you expect to find now?" Judge Saxton asked.

"I don't know," Mason said. "I think the place should be searched."

"Well, if you want to do it and are willing to put up the money as a deposit for electric current, the Court is certainly going to give you that privilege. It is approaching the hour of noon adjournment. The Court will adjourn until two-thirty this afternoon, at which time, Mr. Mason, you will be asked to appear in order to show cause why you should not be found guilty of contempt of court."

"Very well, Your Honor," Mason said. "I will ask the co-operation of the police department in getting immediate service in hooking up the meter on that establishment."

"But this is all foolishness," Hamilton Burger protested. "There is nothing there now. There never was anything there that—"

"How do you know?" Judge Saxton interrupted.

"I know because I know what the human probabilities are."

"This Court is not dealing with human probabilities," Judge Saxton said. "This Court is dealing with the constitutional rights of a defendant charged with crime.

"There is, of course, a tendency when one is searching for something which he expects to find, to discontinue the search when he finds what he has expected. Apparently, that was done in this case. I am not censuring the police. I am simply stating that if the defendant wants the place searched at this time, the Court is not only willing to co-operate in that, but the Court would like to have such a search made.

"The Court instructs the prosecution to co-operate in every way with the defense attorney in getting electricity turned on there.—As I understand it, there will be ample illumination if the electricity is turned on."

Hamilton Burger glanced at Tragg.

"Oh, yes, Your Honor," Tragg said. "There were long fluorescent light tubes in the warehouse and also in the storeroom."

"Very well," Judge Saxton said, "Court will recess until two-thirty this afternoon, and if that isn't sufficient time for the light to have been turned on and a search to be made, the Court will take a further adjournment until tomorrow morning. The present order is that Court is recessed until two-thirty."

Mason moved over to Paul Drake.

"Paul, you're going without lunch."

"I guess everybody's going without lunch," Drake said. "Our next meal may be in jail."

"Forget it," Mason told him. "I want you, during the noon recess, to cover every main bank in town, not the branch banks, but the main banks, and see if ten years ago a deposit of forty-seven thousand dollars in cash was made by mail."

"They aren't going to give that information," Drake said, "even if they know. They—"

"They'll know," Mason said. "You don't get a forty-seven-thousand-dollar cash deposit by mail every day in the week. They may not want to give out the information as to details. Tell them simply we want to know whether such a deposit was received. Put enough men on it to cover the city in the shortest time possible. Get on the telephone, tell them who you are, tell them it's in the interest of justice.''

Drake said moodily, "I was watching Judge Saxton's face when that stuff came out about tampering with the witnesses. That old boy is dead against you, Perry. He's going to throw the book at you.''

Mason grinned and said, "That doesn't mean I can't dodge.''

"Well, you'd better do some pretty fast dodging because I think that old boy is a pretty good pitcher.''

"We aren't licked yet,'' Mason said.

"Well, I don't know what you're trying to prove. My own idea is we're so far behind the eight ball that we aren't ever going to get out.''

Mason said, "Look, Paul, a man gets out of federal prison, he has government agents shadowing him, he has rough shadows and smooth shadows. The guy buys good clothes, he buys good cigars. Where does he get the money?''

"Where indeed?'' Drake asked. "He bought an automobile and he got that money from you.''

"That's right,'' Mason said. "He did that for the moral effect, but when he got the automobile he was all prepared to disappear. He didn't charter a taxi, he didn't have another automobile staked out. The next time we find him he's in a storeroom which has been vacant for some time, which is tied up in litigation, and the storeroom is provisioned with food, a sleeping bag, a suitcase with clothes. Now, where did Collister Gideon get all those things?"

"In stores, probably, he had money."

"He was keeping out of sight," Mason said. "There's more to the Gideon case than we realized."

"Okay, okay," Drake said, "I'll get busy with the banks. Do you want me to try and join you at the storeroom?"

"No," Mason said, "I'm going to goad the police into making the right kind of a search."

Chapter Twenty

THE MAN from the power company said, "Okay, the power's on."

Tragg threw a switch which turned on a battery of lights in the storeroom and office part of the building.

Mason looked around, then moved over to the far side of the room and started a minute search.

Tragg, Hamilton Burger and two plain-clothes men, obviously bored by the entire procedure, looked at their watches, casually looked around and waited for Mason to finish.

"All right, Tragg," Mason said, "here's the first thing I want to look at."

"What's that?"

Mason pointed to a transverse beam over the doorway. "There's something in there. A hole, there's a fresh splinter by the side of the hole."

Tragg started to say something, then changed his mind and said to one of the men, "See if there's a stepladder around here."

Hamilton Burger said, "This is another good

old-fashioned razzle-dazzle. This building hasn't been sealed up. Anyone could have gone in here and planted all sorts of evidence."

Tragg said nothing.

Mason started up on the stepladder. Tragg gently pulled him back and said, "I'll do this, if you don't mind, Perry."

Tragg got up, looked at the hole in the beam, pursed his lips, looked down at Hamilton Burger and said, "I think it's a bullet."

Burger's face flushed. "All right," he said, "we're having Mason up for contempt of court at two-thirty this afternoon on one charge. We may as well have him on two charges. Let's get the bullet out. The same old gag of planting evidence."

"If you folks had made the careful search you should have, it would have been impossible for anyone to have planted evidence," Mason said. "Now we can't tell when that bullet was fired in there."

"Well, I can tell," Hamilton Burger said, "and I can tell who held the gun."

"Want to make a statement in the presence of witnesses so I can hold you liable?" Mason asked.

Hamilton Burger turned his back and walked off.

"In getting that bullet out," Mason said, "please be very careful not to disturb the striations or mark the lead—"

"You don't need to tell me how to take out a bullet," Tragg said.

Tragg enlarged the hole slightly with a pocketknife and said to one of the plain-clothes men. "That's as deep as I can go with a knife. Go out to the car and get that kit that has the drill in it for taking out a section of wood."

The plain-clothes officer returned from the car with an auger designed to cut a circular core from a section of wood.

Tragg said, "Get up there and be very, very careful to be sure you're on the course of that bullet. Cut out a section of the wood that has the bullet in it."

The man climbed the stepladder and, after a few minutes, brought down a section of the wooden beam.

Tragg carefully split the section and shook out the .38-caliber bullet into his hand.

"All right," he said, "we've found the bullet, what do we do next?"

"We have it appraised by Redfield," Mason said.

"All right," Tragg said, "let's get going. I presume you want to have the report before two-thirty?"

"Send a man with the bullet," Mason said. "Let's not make the same mistake twice. Let's not quit searching just because we find something. Let's look this thing over carefully."

"All right," Tragg said, "we'll go into the warehouse now."

They went back in the warehouse. Tragg threw a switch, and the gloomy, dank interior of the place instantly became flooded with light.

"Now, let's take a look around here," Mason said. "Have your men turn over every one of those big cartons and let's see what we can find."

"There are fifty of them here," Tragg said.

"All right," Mason said, "if you can't turn over fifty cartons by two-thirty, we'll telephone the judge and get an order."

"Oh, go ahead," Tragg said.

Tragg and one of the officers shook the corrugated board packing cases one at a time, moved them, looked inside.

Suddenly one of the men started to say something to Tragg, caught himself, looked significantly at the police lieutenant and turned his back.

"What is it?" Mason asked sharply. "We're making this search under an order of court. We're entitled to know."

"Somebody stood in here," the officer said. "You can see the imprint of his rubber heels. They'd been in oil somewhere and they left a print here."

"That doesn't mean a thing," Hamilton Burger said. "You can't tell when the heel prints were made. They could have been made a month ago, or," he added significantly, "they could have been made last night."

"Nevertheless," Mason, said, "they were made. It's evidence. Let's take the packing case into custody."

"All right," Tragg said wearily, "take it along."

"And I want it dusted for fingerprints."

"You can't get fingerprints from paper— Oh, well, let him have his way. Leave it here long enough for a technical man to come down and dust for fingerprints. What else do you want, Mason?"

"I don't know," Mason said, moving slowly around, prowling into the various nooks and corners of the place.

Suddenly Mason said, "Hey, wait a minute, this window has been forced."

"I should have guessed that a long while ago," Hamilton Burger said. "That's how the man got in to fire the bullet into that beam."

"This window has been opened from the inside," Mason said. "You see, the cobwebs have been brushed away and the window was opened, then lowered. It's unlocked."

"An inside-outside job," Hamilton Burger said. "Same old razzle-dazzle."

Tragg studied the pane thoughtfully.

"Now, wait a minute," Mason said. "What's this?"

"What?" Tragg asked.

Mason pointed over to a corner. "I got a glint of reflected light from blued steel."

Tragg moved over, said, "Oh, oh, it's a gun!"

Hamilton Burger started to say something, then checked himself and said, "All right, it's a gun. Take it into custody, Lieutenant, and we'll have it examined carefully in court. We'll see whose fingerprints we find on it—although the person who planted it there was probably shrewd enough to wear gloves."

Mason said, "Be careful with it, Lieutenant, and I want some test bullets fired from it. You will note that that also is a thirty-eight-caliber Smith and Wesson."

"It would be," Hamilton Burger said.

"Meaning," Mason said casually, "that in your opinion it was planted."

"It *was* planted," Hamilton Burger said angrily. "And at two-thirty this afternoon I hope to be able to show who did the planting."

"You wouldn't want to make any accusations before then, would you?" Mason asked.

"I have my opinion," Burger said, turning away.

"You have everything you want?" Tragg asked.

"I don't know," Mason said. "I want this place sealed up; put an officer in charge and leave him here until we can evaluate this evidence we have at the present time."

"Okay, okay," Tragg said. "I want to see if there are any fingerprints on that gun but ordinarily we don't get fingerprints on guns. Sometimes you get a thumbprint at the base of a cartridge clip, but it's not once in a hundred that you get a fingerprint off a gun."

"All right, we've got the gun," Mason said. "I want Redfield to fire test bullets through it. I'd like to have him bring his comparison microscope into court so we can make tests right there in court."

"The good old drama," Hamilton Burger said. "Never forget the dramatic approach. That's showmanship. I'm getting damned sick and tired of all this. Every case we have, it's the same old razzle-dazzle, the same old seven and six."

Mason looked at his watch and said, "If you'd hurry, Hamilton, you might be able to get some lunch; at least a cup of coffee, and I think it's possible that would change your outlook."

Chapter Twenty-One

AT TWO-THIRTY, Judge Saxton, who had conceivably heard some rumors of what had happened, took the bench with a glance of puzzled respect at Perry Mason.

"Search of the premises has been completed in the case of People versus Warren?" he asked.

"No, Your Honor," Mason said, "but a search has been made and that search has uncovered certain things. I believe Lieutenant Tragg was on the stand and he can probably testify as to what was discovered."

"Very well. Lieutenant Tragg to the stand," Judge Saxton said.

Mason said, "I believe I was cross-examining Lieutenant Tragg, but I don't know that it makes much difference who brings this out. . . . Lieutenant, you found certain things in the storeroom at Clovina and Hendersell?"

"We did," Tragg said, dryly.

"What did you find?"

"When the lights were turned on, we found

that a beam over the door between the storeroom and the warehouse had a bullet which had lodged in it. We took that bullet out without destroying any of the striations or leaving any tool marks on it. I have that bullet here.''

"Will you mark it for identification, please, as Defendant's Exhibit Number 1a?''

"It will be so marked for identification,'' Judge Saxton said.

"What else did you find?''

"We found a Smith and Wesson thirty-eight-caliber revolver containing five live shells and one exploded cartridge.''

"Have you tested that gun?''

"I understand that Alexander Redfield has fired a test bullet through it. To that extent the gun has been tested.''

"And,'' Mason asked, "didn't Alexander Redfield compare the test bullet from that gun with the fatal bullet in this case?''

"I believe he did, yes, sir.''

"That test was in your presence?''

"Yes, sir.''

"And did Alexander Redfield state to you what he had found?''

"Objected to as hearsay,'' Hamilton Burger said.

"Sustained,'' Judge Saxton said. "You can put Mr. Redfield on the stand. In fact you can put him on for further cross-examination if you wish.''

"Now, then,'' Mason said, "during all of the

time that you were at the scene of the murder and while you were finding these things, was Hamilton Burger, the district attorney, present?"

"Why, yes, he was."

"And did he keep up a running fire of remarks indicating that I had planted this evidence?"

"I'll stipulate that I did," Hamilton Burger said angrily.

"There you are," Mason said, turning to Judge Saxton. "Lieutenant Tragg is a witness in this case, and during the entire course of our search, the district attorney was belittling the objects we found, was implanting in the mind of this witness the idea that I had been responsible for having those objects at the scene of the crime, that the evidence was without proper evidentiary value and had been planted.

"If the Court please, if I am to be cited to show cause for contempt of court for seeking to influence the testimony of a witness, I insist that the district attorney also be cited at the same time for seeking to influence the testimony of this witness."

Judge Saxton looked at the angry district attorney, at Lt. Tragg and then tried to fight back a smile.

"Very well, Mr. Mason," he said, "the Court will note your motion. However, that doesn't mean the Court will act on it. Let's proceed with the evidence in this case."

"I want my motion to show that the district attorney was there in his official capacity, that his remarks carried all the weight of an elected official of this county who conceivably had influence over the police department, that they represented a continual running fire of accusation."

"Very well, we will take that up at the proper time," Judge Saxton said. "I presume now you would like to call Mr. Redfield to the stand."

"I would, Your Honor."

"I note Mr. Redfield is in court," Judge Saxton said. "You may take the stand, Mr. Redfield."

Mason said, "If the Court please, this comes under the heading of further cross-examination.

"Mr. Redfield, you stated that, taking *all* the facts into consideration and in all human probability, the gun, People's Exhibit B, was the weapon from which the fatal bullet had been fired. I'm now going to ask you if, since the time you gave your testimony, subsequent facts have been disclosed which change your opinion?"

"They have."

"Now, then, taking into consideration *all* the facts, are you still willing to swear that in all human probability, the fatal bullet was fired from the gun, People's Exhibit B?"

"No, I am not," Redfield said. "In fact, I am now prepared to swear positively that the gun which was discovered this noon at the scene of the murder and which is now labeled for identification as Defendant's Exhibit Number 1a was the gun from which the fatal bullet was fired."

"What!" Judge Saxton asked, unable to

conceal his surprise.

"Yes, Your Honor. I am sorry, but enough striations are visible on the base of the fatal bullet so that it is possible to make a match. It isn't easy, but there is enough of a match so that I am now satisfied that the fatal bullet was fired from this gun, Defendant's Exhibit 1a."

"Now, then," Mason said, "are you also prepared to make a statement in regard to the bullet which was found in the beam over the door?"

"Yes, sir."

"What gun was that fired from?"

"That was fired from the gun, People's Exhibit B."

"So," Mason said, "with only one shot fired from that gun, People's Exhibit Number B, we now have that bullet accounted for as having been fired into a beam. Therefore that gun couldn't possibly have been used in the commission of the crime. Is that right?"

"Scientifically, and in my opinion as an expert, that is correct," Redfield said.

Judge Saxton threw his hands apart in a gesture which a man makes when he is tossing something away.

"Now, then," Mason said, "I have one more request to make. Your office keeps a record of fatal bullets and unsolved crimes?"

"Yes, it does."

"I am referring now to the attempted murder of the watchman at the Pacific Northern

Supermarket," Mason said. "You have the bullet that was recovered from his body?"

"Yes."

"I asked you to bring it with you. Will you make a comparison test on the microscope and tell me whether you can match that bullet with the test bullet which was fired from Defendant's Exhibit Number 1a?"

"Since you asked me to bring that bullet into court, I knew what you had in mind," Redfield said, somewhat wearily, "and I have made such a test."

"With what result?"

"The bullet that wounded the watchman was also fired from this gun which has been marked for identification as Defendant's Exhibit Number 1a."

Mason turned to Judge Saxton. "There you are, Your Honor. I had deduced from the evidence that the decedent had committed a holdup at the Pacific Northern Supermarket. I had a sketch made of the decedent and approached the eyewitnesses with such a sketch. Then the district attorney of this county, using the weight of his high office, led the witnesses to believe that I had unduly influenced them, thereby ruining their testimony so that it can't be used in an attempted murder case. I suggest, if the Court please, that in addition to asking that the district attorney be cited for contempt in influencing the testimony of Lieutenant Tragg, that he also be cited for contempt in influencing the testimony of two witnesses who saw the holdup man at the scene of the crime at the Pacific Northern Supermarket, and by the use of his influence, his skepticism and the power of suggestion so changed their identification that it would now be useless to attempt to prove the crime committed by the decedent."

Judge Saxton looked at Hamilton Burger's utterly astounded countenance, at Redfield, at Lt. Tragg and said, suddenly, "It appears that as far as the case against this defendant is concerned, there is none. All that can be brought to bear against him is that he was hiding at the scene of the crime. That certainly is not enough to warrant this Court in binding the defendant over. The Court, therefore, is going to dismiss the case against the defendant, and as far as all these other incidental matters of contempt are concerned, the Court is going to strike them off the calendar and give the matter consideration and announce whether there will be a hearing at some later date.

"Court's adjourned."

Chapter Twenty-Two

As HAMILTON BURGER stalked angrily from the courtroom, Lt. Tragg came over and gave Mason the benefit of his whimsical smile.

"Well, Perry," he said, "we all of us make mistakes. Every once in a while I deviate from good old-fashioned police procedure because I think I have everything I need and every once in a while I find I'm on the wrong side of the fence.

"I certainly should have had the lights turned on and searched that place. Now then, how did you deduce what happened?"

Mason said, "I began to feel that Gideon had an accomplice. I think that accomplice was someone whom he met in prison. There wasn't an opportunity for him to have an accomplice otherwise. It must have been someone who was in prison and who was released within probably the first year after Gideon was incarcerated."

"But why would they have an association which would endure all that time, and—"

Mason said, "Here's Paul Drake coming now. I

think he has the answer."

Paul Drake, hurrying into the courtroom, looked at the sprinkling of startled spectators talking in knots, at the empty bench where Judge Saxton should have been sitting, then hurried over to Mason and Lt. Tragg. "What happened?" he asked. "What happened?"

Della Street said, "The judge dismissed the case."

"Dismissed it?" Drake echoed.

"That's right," Mason said. "Quite a few things happened this noon. What did you find out about the money, Paul?"

"You were dead right. A deposit of forty-seven thousand dollars was made by mail. Just plain mail. The money was in an envelope with postage on it and nothing else. Naturally it aroused a lot of curiosity.

"There have been no withdrawals, but at regular intervals since, small sums of money have been deposited to the account, so that it kept the account listed on the bank's records as a live account."

"And the name of the man who deposited the account?" Mason asked.

"Collister Damon," Drake said. "And, of course, I only need remind you that Gideon's full name was Collister Damon Gideon.

"He undoubtedly had an accomplice who was released from prison shortly after he was incarcerated. That person couldn't draw *out* the money, because he couldn't establish his identity

229

as Collister Damon, but anyone can make deposits to an account and once deposits are made the account continues to be a live account.''

A plain-clothes man hurried into the courtroom and motioned to Tragg.

Tragg said, "Excuse me," went to talk with him, came back and said, "Well, Perry, I guess we've got the clues we need. Somebody had been touching an object that was greasy and when he jumped into that corrugated packing box he left fingerprints, enough so that they can be identified. Now then, we'll go over the records of prisoners who were released from the federal penitentiary where Gideon was confined and see what we can find there.''

"Good enough," Mason said.

"Perhaps you can tell me what happened between Gideon and the accomplice?" Tragg said.

"Sure," Mason said, "it's only surmise but I think you'll find it'll work out once you get the accomplice.

"They had a nice hide-out here in this deserted store. I think you'll find the fingerprints of this accomplice on some of the cooking utensils and empty tin cans.''

Tragg winced and said, "Let's not rub it in, Perry.''

"And," Mason went on, "they were getting by all right until things went wrong and Gideon shot this night watchman. He lost his head completely. That put the accomplice in the position of having a possible one-way ticket to the gas chamber.

Whenever two or more persons commit a felony, and a murder is committed in connection with the felony, all of them are equally guilty of first-degree murder. For all they knew, the watchman was going to die.

"All of a sudden Gideon became hotter than a stove lid. He wanted out of town. He didn't dare, under the circumstances, to try and draw that money out of the bank. He needed money and he needed it bad. He put the bite on me. He put the bite on Warren."

"Can you tell me what he had on you and what he had on Warren?" Tragg asked.

"No, I can't," Mason said, "and it would help a lot if you'd not try to find out. You don't need to, you know."

"Probably not," Tragg said.

"Anyway, Warren let the gun out of his possession. Gideon had a fight with his accomplice and Gideon tried to kill him. Gideon missed. The accomplice didn't."

Tragg said, "Why should Warren have conveniently left the gun for Gideon to pick up? He— Now wait a minute, Gideon was putting the bite on everybody he could."

Tragg's eyes narrowed. "I wonder if by any chance Mrs. Warren was included in his list of victims. I wonder if she went down there with a gun and then Warren came in later. He found Gideon dead with the gun nearby and Warren picked up the gun, so as to protect his wife, pocketed it and was trying to make his escape when he heard sirens tearing down the street and assumed it was the police."

Mason met Tragg's eyes. "Those," he said, "are the things I wish you wouldn't try to speculate about, Tragg. The accomplice will state that he killed Gideon in self-defense and I think perhaps he's right. Gideon shot at him with the Warren gun. The accomplice retaliated with the gun they had been using in their holdups—the gun Gideon had had on the night the supermarket was held up."

Tragg was thoughtfully silent.

"That's all you need," Mason said. "The federal boys can recover the forty-seven thousand dollars and there's nothing left for you to worry about."

"But you want to keep your clients out of this?"

Mason met his eyes, "I want to keep my clients out of it."

Silently, Tragg extended his hand and shook hands. "You've been a big help, Perry," he said. "I don't suppose you could go a step farther and give us some clue as to the identity of the accomplice, could you?"

"Why not?" Mason asked.

Tragg raised his eyebrows.

"Think it over," Mason said. "I had a sketch made of Collister Gideon. We know now that he was connected with that holdup and shooting at the supermarket.

"The night watchman who was wounded

unhesitatingly identified the Gideon sketch as having a resemblance to the man who had done the shooting.

"The other witness was positive that the sketch didn't look like the man who had run out of the door. Yet it was the man who ran out of the door who had the gun."

Tragg said thoughtfully, "There could have been *two* men connected with the holdup."

Mason grinned, "And the police found a man running down the street. If the man had tried to hide, they'd have grabbed him and charged him with being the accomplice, but because the man had enough presence of mind to run out in the middle of the street and start waving his arms at the police car trying to flag it down, the police fell for the strategy and—"

"Good God!" Tragg interpolated. "Do you mean Drew Kearny was the accomplice?"

"Of course he was the accomplice," Mason said. "That's why he wouldn't identify Gideon. He didn't dare to. He didn't want Gideon to have any connection with that supermarket. He was hoping that the police would never find the gun he had left in the old warehouse after the shooting.

"Kearny is clever as hell and a consummate actor. Take his fingerprints. Shake him down and you'll find he has a criminal record, that he was in federal prison for a while when Collister Gideon was there, that Gideon confided in him, that Kearny came to this town, established a small business which gave him a legitimate front. From time to time he made deposits on the forty-seven-thousand-dollar account Gideon had established. He was waiting for the time when Gideon would be released and could draw checks on the account without having the authorities censoring his mail.

"Kearny is probably responsible for a whole chain of burglaries that the police would like to clear up. He was smart enough, however, to know that he had to keep his criminal activities entirely divorced from his legitimate activities; therefore he had a hide-out he had established in this old deserted building which was tied up in litigation. He would stay there when he wanted to pull a job. Probably his jobs were pulled, for the most part, on weekends.— Of course I'm going on guesswork and probabilities, Lieutenant, but there's no other explanation for that holdup gun being the fatal gun which killed Gideon, and Kearny just had to be the accomplice on that supermarket job. That's why he was running down the street, not *toward* the telephone, but *away* from the scene of the crime."

Tragg heaved a deep sigh. "Where would you have been if Kearny had got back to that warehouse and removed that gun before we found it?" Tragg asked.

Mason looked at his watch. "Probably being sentenced for contempt of court right now," he said.

"Then you weren't influencing the witness at all," Tragg said. "The witness was drawing red herrings across the trail just as fast as he could."

"And because the watchman said the sketch of Gideon did look like the man he had surprised in the supermarket, the district attorney and the police were blaming me for having influenced the other guy's testimony," Mason said.

Abruptly Tragg threw back his head, laughed, and said, "Well, I guess we'll get busy on a roundup, Perry."

"Going to take Hamilton Burger in on it?" Mason asked.

Tragg said, "I think I'll keep out of Burger's office for a few hours, if you don't mind, Perry."

"I don't mind in the least," Mason told him.

A note on the text
Large print edition designed by
Fred Welden.
Composed in 16 pt English Times
on an EditWriter 7700
by Cheryl Yodlin of G.K. Hall Corp.